The One I Didn't See Coming

PIPER RAYNE

Cover Design: By Hang Le

1st Line Editor: Joy Editing

2nd Line Editor: My Brother's Editor

Proofreader: My Brother's Editor

About The One I Didn't See Coming

It's the classic story—girl returns to her hometown only to end up moving in with her high school crush, who she hates.

Returning to Willowbrook was my only option after Chicago chewed me up and spit me out. Technically, it wasn't Chicago's fault. It was *his* fault—the man I thought I knew who turned out to be a liar.

My older sister, always the one to swoop in and fix things, secured me a job as a yoga instructor on her fiancé's family ranch. As my self-assigned protector, she's keeping one eye on me and one eye on Emmett Noughton, her fiancé's brother.

He's the charming, fun-loving, take-life-as-it-comes kind of guy, and once upon a time, his name was scribbled in my notebooks. Back then, I was invisible to him. Now, he's looking at me like I'm the only thing in the room. But he lost his chance with me a long time ago.

It's easy to keep him at arm's length and nurse the grudge I've held onto for years. Until the house I'm staying in sells, and I have nowhere to go except his house. Now, resisting him isn't just difficult—it's impossible.

THE ONE I *Didn't See Coming*

Plain Daisy Ranch Family

The Noughton Family

Parents

Bruce and Daisy (deceased) Noughton

Children

Ben Noughton – Gillian Adams

(*The One I Left Behind*)

Jude Noughton – Sadie Wilkins

(*The One I Stood Beside*)

Emmett Noughton – Briar Adams

(*The One I Didn't See Coming*)

The Owens Family

Parents

Brad and Darla Owens

Children

Lottie Owens

Bennett Owens

Romy Owens

The Ellis Family

Parents

Wade and Bette Ellis

Children

Poppy Ellis

Jensen Ellis

Scarlett Ellis

To see more of the Plain Daisy Ranch

family tree visit our website:
https://piperrayne.com/noughton-family-tree

Chapter One

EMMETT

I leave the bathroom and jog down the stairs, overhearing my brother Jude talking to Dad in the kitchen. Dad decided to ambush us today, asking all of us to meet at his house.

We all know it's about business because first, he's making his famous burgers, which he only cooks when he's trying to get my two brothers and me to agree on something. Second, it's for sure about business because if our family meeting was about anything other than business, it'd be held up on daisy hill at Mom's burial plot.

None of us want to be here. Ben groaned because he didn't want to be away from his soon-to-be bride for longer than a minute. Jude bitched because we all know what this meeting is about, and he's been delaying it for months.

"You have no choice. I promise you that when the baby comes, you'll want more time at home. Sadie will need you." A kitchen chair screeches against the vinyl floor.

"But, Dad—"

I walk into the kitchen, interrupting them, but neither

one bats an eye because my family doesn't keep many secrets—or can't keep any secrets, more like it.

"Are we still trying to get Jude to give up the reins?" I grab a water from the fridge and smirk at Jude just to piss him off. It's an easy task any day, but especially today. You'd think I was some up-and-comer trying to take over his cushy job the way he protects his responsibilities on the ranch like a growling dog anchoring his jaw in his pull toy.

I don't *want* his position on the family ranch.

"Hey, did I tell you we're way past a million views on your baby girl's gender reveal video?" I flip the chair around and straddle it.

"Sit right, Emmett," my dad scolds.

What's up his ass?

"Act like you're ready," he adds.

Ding, ding, ding. There's the reason he's suddenly giving me hell about how I sit in a chair.

"Should I go put on the suit I wear to funerals? Want to know my strengths and weaknesses? We can have a formal interview if you like."

Dad inhales deeply through his nose.

Ben walks in the back door like a damn stealth bomber. "How long is this going to take?"

"Shit," Jude says, jolting back in his chair.

"Just sit down. I'm not sure why I have to bribe you all to have a meeting regarding the ranch." Dad puts down a plate of burgers in the middle of the table.

He'll probably never give us the secret to what he puts in the meat, but damn, he makes the best burgers. After Mom died, it was all he made for a long time, but we never grew sick of them, which is a testament to how good they are.

We all reach in, hands smacking hands, hands pushing hands out of the way to score as many as we can.

"Thanks, Dad," Jude mumbles and moans over his first bite.

"You should quit the ranch and open a burger joint," I say.

"You'd have a line around the block," Ben says.

All of us take huge bites as if we haven't eaten in a week.

"Kind words from some boys who are afraid of why I called them here." Dad sits back, his burger on his plate, watching us.

He does this every once in a while—watches us. I've never asked why, but I think he's impressed he raised us on his own, for the most part, and we're not jackasses. Well, most of the time we're not.

"Eat, Dad." Ben nudges his arm.

"I will."

Jude finishes first—which is why he had the nickname garbage disposal when we were younger. He was always the first to the table, no matter the meal, and the first finished. "So, why are we here, other than…"

"Me taking over Jude's position." I smile wide and wink at Jude.

He blows out an annoyed breath, his usual reaction to my razzing. "You're not taking my position."

"Are you sure about that?" Ben joins in on the fun.

The problem with having three boys is that it's always two against one.

"You can all fuck off. Dad?" Jude pulls out his phone and looks at the time. "Sadie is expecting me."

"There's plenty to take home." Dad glances toward the Tupperware containers on the counter.

"Another good thing about not having a woman—I get another burger meal for myself." I smile at the three of them.

"And the use of your hand tonight while Jude and I will be snug inside—"

"Enough," Dad says. "Don't talk like that in front of me. I'm not your buddy at the bar, and the women in your houses are like daughters to me. I don't want to think or visualize..." He shakes his head. "Just. No." He gives Ben his look. The one he mastered after Mom died, and he had to raise three hellions on his own.

Ben holds up his hands. "All right."

"The reason I called you here is because yes, Sadie is getting closer to bringing the first Noughton grandchild into the world—"

"You're welcome." Jude holds out his arms, pointing at himself as if there should be a big J on his chest.

"It should've happened years ago," Ben mumbles, snagging one of the last two burgers.

I reach to grab the last one at the same time as Jude.

"You get the first child, I get the last burger." I swipe it off the plate before he can. Satisfaction fills my chest. Nothing better than beating my brothers at... well, anything.

"Had enough? You're the reason this meeting is taking so damn long." Dad eyes each of us, and we sober as we usually do under his scrutiny. "Like I was saying. It's almost planting season, so that's where we start."

My stomach rolls over, and I almost slide off the chair and go back to the bathroom, but I gave myself a mental pep talk upstairs before coming down here. I can do this, even if I'm sure I already know what their reaction will be.

I put my burger down. "Actually, I was thinking—"

"Realized what that brain is for, huh?" Ben jokes, and Jude laughs along with him.

I raise my middle finger and run it up and down my nose as if I'm scratching it.

"So, Jude, you'll teach Emmett everything that needs to happen to get the corn planted, and then we'll move on to the cattle ranch. You're still responsible for the horses, Emmett."

I raise my hand, earning groans from both Ben and Jude.

"It's not kindergarten," Dad says. "Speak."

"I had this idea that maybe we could open a dude ranch." I spit out my idea before I'm interrupted. I want to make my own mark on this ranch, not be Jude's gofer my entire life.

"Dude ranch? Like people would come here to work?" Ben laughs and knocks his elbow against Jude's arm.

"I know it's not *your* dream vacation, but we have so much to offer here." I slide my phone out of my pocket. "On the gender reveal video—"

"If I hear the words gender reveal video one more time, I'm gonna lose the three burgers I just ate." Jude swipes his drink off the table and downs half the glass.

I ignore him because he's always a negative Nancy. "All these people commented asking where the ranch is and if they could come visit."

"But none of them are saying they want to work?" Ben asks.

"Some are. They want to come and see how things work, see me on a horse and stuff."

Ben slaps his hands together. "And there it is. Emmett wants to show off."

"Excuse me, Mr. Running Back," I say, annoyed that none of them are taking me seriously.

"I wasn't showing off, I was playing to win." Ben rolls his eyes.

"Yeah, okay."

My brother liked the attention, and at one point in his career, he liked it so much my dad had to fly out and straighten him out.

"Anyway, it sounds like it could be a good idea, Emmett, but right now, we have to get you up to speed on the ranch before we can entertain something new. Tell them where we are, and they can stay at The Getaway Lodge, go on a winery tour, or something." Dad grabs our plates. "You can go about your nights now." He stands.

"That's it?" I ask.

Ben slides out of his chair, smacks Dad on the back, and grabs the doggie bag Dad made up for Gillian and his stepson, Clayton. "Gillian probably won't see any of these. Thanks."

"I put an extra one in there for Clayton. He's growing." Dad heads over to the sink to wash the dishes.

"And bonus, I get sex and another burger because Sadie is having an adverse reaction to beef these days." Jude holds up his bag, trying to coax me into battle, but I'm not going to bite.

"Yeah, I can get sex if I want it *and* the burger. The best thing is that I don't have to wake up next to them in the morning." I pick up my bag. "Can we talk about the dude ranch some more?"

"That's the difference between us—we want them there in the morning." Ben smiles. "One day you'll grow up."

Ben pats me on the back and smiles at Jude as if he's inviting him to join in on the fun. I hate that they throw their relationships in my face as though I'm jealous. I'm totally not. What I am is aggravated that everyone, including my dad, disregarded my idea about the dude ranch so easily.

When Jude doesn't say anything, Ben says, "Don't forget everyone, we'll be inviting an extra person to Sunday dinner at my house."

Everyone's eyes shift to me because Ben's been telling us for days that Gillian's half sister, Briar, is coming back to Willowbrook.

"What?" I ask, as though they're warning me off her for no reason.

Ben points at me. "Hands off. Seriously, she's your sister."

My dad ignores us, cleaning the dishes.

"Not sure you understand how it works, bro. Briar is definitely *not* my sister."

"She's living at Gillian's until the house sells, and she's here to teach yoga, so keep your focus on the ranch and away from the studio." Ben eyes me as if I'm scared of him.

"From what I got at the softball games last fall, Briar doesn't much care for our little brother. Isn't that right, Little Noughton?" Jude clasps my shoulder.

He's right. Briar has come back to Willowbrook a couple of times since then, and each time, she's meaner than the last. I'm not sure what I did to piss her off.

"She'll like me soon enough." I wink at Ben, and he growls.

"Don't lay one finger on her. It's not only me but also Gillian you have to worry about."

"Gilly Bean is as scary as a goldfish, and sorry to tell you this, but unless you plan on locking Briar in a basement, the men in Willowbrook will notice her. She's all grown up."

It's the truth. Briar Adams is fucking hot, but I'm only saying this to piss Ben off and make him think I'm going to flirt with and maybe sleep with her. Which I would never do because who needs that kind of drama in their life? I can get laid elsewhere.

"Enough, boys. Go. I have things to do." Dad shoos us out, soap suds dripping from his hand.

We each thank Dad for dinner.

"Guys, I'm serious about this dude ranch thing," I say as we walk down the dirt road toward our houses that line up along the lake.

"At the moment you're serious about it," Ben says.

My hands clench at my sides.

"Dad's right. After we get you running more of the ranch, you can make a business plan." Jude turns to the right to head toward his house. He waves his goodbye. "See you."

"Ben?" I arch an eyebrow, hopeful he'll reconsider and take me seriously.

He looks over his shoulder. This is where he turns off from me. "You know I don't have much to do with the ranch. I'm a football coach, Emmett."

"But—"

He's gone, though, starting toward his house. I stop walking, rock my head back, and stare at the dark, star-filled sky.

A car pulls down the road that goes past our houses, but Ben stops it before it reaches me. Inside I can just make out the blonde who has been sneaking her way into my beat-off sessions lately. So she's back in Willowbrook for a longer visit this time? Must be if she's going to be teaching yoga on the ranch.

My dick twitches, so I look down and shake my head. "Sorry, big guy, she's off-limits."

Sucks that there's nothing I love better than a challenge. Which is why I walk toward the headlights when I should run away from them.

Chapter Two

BRIAR

I know I'm on the Plain Daisy Ranch, but other than that, I'm lost.

My car rounds a corner, and my headlights shine down the small one-way road that supposedly leads to Ben and Gillian's house, which they just built. However, I don't see any houses other than the white family house I passed after driving under the arches.

I stop and turn on the interior light, then try to find my phone in my purse to call my sister and ask for more specific instructions other than to turn left after the fourth tree that's missing a limb. But my phone must have fallen out and slid under the seat when I had to slam on the brakes when a deer ran out onto the road.

I'm sure I passed their drive, but I'm not sure I can just turn around without going off the road, and since it's dark, I'm not one hundred percent sure I won't go into a ditch or something. I put the car in drive and press on the gas, but a big figure shines in the headlights with his hand held up.

I slam on the brakes. "Shit."

Ben taps the hood of the car and walks around to the

driver's side with that easy smile of his. Must be nice to have everything you ever dreamed of in your life. Farther down the road is another broad figure, and my stomach clenches.

Emmett Noughton, the party boy, take-life-as-it-comes, immature jackass. Why doesn't he just go inside his house?

"Hey, Briar," Ben says, standing outside my window. "Turned around? We're back that way." He points as if that vague direction is clear.

"Yeah, does this drive go all the way around the lake?"

He chuckles. "No. Just to Jude's, and he spooks easily with Sadie being pregnant, so better to stay out of that driveway."

"I don't want to run over the grass," I say, pretending I don't see the tall figure standing in the distance, even though I can feel his eyes on me.

If I gave Emmett the time of day, he'd probably stop acting as though my hatred toward him is some kind of flirtation when it's actually real and true hatred.

Ben looks around at either side of us, hemming and hawing. He turns toward Emmett and mumbles something under his breath. "Yeah, go down to the next drive and turn around. Then we'll get you to the house." His shoulders sink.

I point in front of me. "That way?" He can't be serious.

"Yeah." He releases another deep sigh. "Roll up your windows and lock the doors." His voice is strained, and he doesn't crack a smile.

"Is the boogeyman going to come and get me?"

He mumbles again, but I don't catch it. "Just ignore any of his antics."

I ease off the gas and inch my car toward where Ben wants me to turn around, which I'm guessing is Emmett's place. That's the reason he's still standing there.

Emmett steps to the side of the road as I turn my car into his drive. "Get lost, Goldilocks?"

That's when I remember I never rolled up the window like Ben told me to.

"Wrong story." My hand moves to roll up the window.

He leans in, crossing his arms on the edge of my car door, his head coming past the line of appropriate distance. "But my brothers and I are like the three bears, and only one of us would be just right for you." He grins at me.

I shift the transmission into reverse to get out of here even if I have to run him over. "Red Riding Hood was the one lost in the woods."

"Oh, I like that better. I'm the big bad wolf, and you're the lost innocent girl?"

"You're more like a yappy Chihuahua."

He draws back for a moment. "Honey, I'm a Doberman."

My eyes narrow on him. "I'm curious, what kind of mirrors are in your house?"

He leans in further, closing in on me. "Why? Are you interested in watching me fuck you?"

"For the one whole minute you'd last?" I press my finger on the window button.

"One night with me, and you'd be ruined for life."

"Emmett!" Ben's voice rings out in the night air.

Emmett laughs, having no choice but to step back or get pinched by the window. Once it's closed, I start backing up to turn around, but my passenger car door opens. I slam on the brakes.

Emmett climbs in, placing a bag on the floor by his feet.

"What are you doing?"

"Being a gentleman and showing you the way." His tone is as if he said duh, what do you think I'm doing?

"A gentleman? You?" I put the car in drive to get this over with because I've met men like Emmett, and rarely do they listen to anything but what their tiny little brains tell them to do.

"Yeah." He shrugs and points ahead of him. "Continue this way."

"No shit."

He rolls down the window, and when we get to Ben, I stop. Emmett hangs out of the window, both arms stretched toward the ground. "I'll show her the way. See you there."

"Bullshit." Ben moves for the handle of my two-door car, and Emmett slaps it away, locking the car manually.

"Emmett, I'm tired, and I don't wanna deal with your shit today," Ben says.

I've never heard Ben with so much anger or annoyance in his tone. Then again, I only briefly knew him when I was younger, and he dated Gillian. They reunited after he returned to Willowbrook when he retired as a pro football player.

"We'll see you at the house," Emmett says. "I'll take good care of my sister."

"Emmett..." Ben's tone is like a warning, but even I know Emmett is going to get off on him being mad.

"Ben," he mimics his brother's tone, rolling up his window. "Go ahead, sweetheart."

"Don't call me that."

Emmett turns toward me, and I purposely drive slowly so Ben can keep up. "Everyone likes me, everyone but you."

"That's what your ego tells you."

His laughter rings out in my small car, grating on my nerves. "Turn right here." He points, and I follow his directions. "You think I have a big ego?"

"You know you have a big ego." I head down a winding road, and the house comes into view. It's big and beautiful and what Gillian's always deserved.

"A big ego to match a big—"

I slam on the brakes, and Emmett catapults forward, hitting his head on the dashboard.

Gillian stands in the middle of the road, her arms crossed.

"Shit." Emmett touches his forehead and pulls his fingers away, examining them as if he expects to find blood.

My sister's eyes are focused solely on Emmett. Then a fist knocks on the window. Ben stands outside.

Emmett opens the car door and steps out. "Damn it, Gilly Bean."

She walks around to Emmett, disregarding him and sliding into the passenger seat before shutting the door and locking it.

"Hey," Gillian says kindly, as though she didn't just resemble a crazy serial killer from the movies about to chop us into pieces.

"Um, hi."

"Go ahead and keep driving. I'll direct you on where to park." She gestures with her hand.

I do as she says because she's always had that disciplinary mom persona. After my mom took off, I knew what Gillian would let me to get away with and what she was really firm on. When she was younger, before she had Clayton, I could manipulate her emotions about not having my mother figure in my life, and she'd loosen the reins on me a little, but those days are long gone.

"Park over there."

I park my car. I didn't really want to come here first when I rolled into town, but Gillian said she wanted to see me and give me the key to her house in town that she's offered to let me stay in until it sells. After that, I'm not sure where I'll go.

We both slide out of the car.

"Go home, Emmett," Ben says as they walk toward the car.

"You're playing two against one, calling Gilly Bean on me." He's still holding his head. What a baby.

"Emmett, I don't have food for you," Gillian says, hooking her arm through mine and leading me toward the stairs.

"I just ate. Which reminds me, I have to get my food out of your car."

"Good, do that, then keep on walking back to your house," Ben says.

"We have a guest. I wanted to welcome her back to Willowbrook."

"You're not the Willowbrook welcome crew," Gillian says over her shoulder, climbing the stairs with me in tow.

"Uncle Emmett!" Clayton comes out of the house and tosses a football to the person closest to his mental age.

"Shit, Clay, give me some warning," Emmett says.

"Thanks, kid," I say and dislodge from Gillian to accost Clayton with a hug.

"Aunt Briar," he whines as I splash kisses all over his face like I used to when he was two years old. "Come on."

"Oh sorry, I heard you had a girlfriend. Is she the only one who can kiss you now?"

He squirms out of my hold.

By the time I'm done, Gillian and Ben are inside arguing about Emmett being here—Ben's saying he can't control his brother, and Gillian's saying he better try. So I'm caught off guard when Emmett overthrows the ball, and Clayton has to jog away to get it.

"Tell me why I'm jealous of a fifteen-year-old boy right now," he whispers in my ear, causing a rush of shivers to race up my spine. Damn him.

"Because you both only think about the same thing every second of every day."

"Come over to my house, and I'll show you exactly what I'm thinking."

"I'm done babysitting five-year-olds," I say, opening the screen door so it hits him square in the nose. "Whoops, sorry about that."

He groans and grabs his nose. "You Adams women are dangerous."

"You're best to remember that." I walk into Gillian's house, hoping like hell Emmett takes the hint and goes home.

If only my mind would shut off the image of him taking me to his house and fucking me while I watch in the mirror. I have way too much going on in my life to entertain any kind of attraction to Emmett Noughton.

Chapter Three

EMMETT

The last thing I want to do on my day off is attend another Sunday night family dinner. After my mom died, the tradition died with her, but now that my brothers have found love, my new sister-in-law and new practically-sister-in-law plan them every week for all of us to catch up.

What do we need to catch up about?

I work with Jude and my dad every damn day on our cattle ranch. When Ben's soon-to-be wife fuels her reality television addiction, he makes my home his.

Recently, Gillian and Sadie, two of the three new additions to the Noughton family, decided our regular Sunday dinners haven't been painful enough, so they added on game night.

I shut my front door, walk down the porch steps, and decide to take my time walking over to Ben's place. If I'm lucky, they'll already be halfway through dinner. Maybe I can say I have a stomachache and sneak out before the game starts.

I love my family. My brothers are my best friends, and you can't ask for better sisters-in-law than Gillian and Sadie. Add on Gillian's son, Clayton, who's always game for throwing around a football, playing a video game, or whatever else we can do to avoid sitting around the table discussing the adult shit, and I've truly won the lottery in terms of family. And not just the scratch-off kind. The big lotto. The one where the jackpot is so big, people travel over state lines to buy tickets. But it doesn't mean I want to spend the last night of every weekend doing family game night.

My family's voices carry through the trees before I round the corner. They're milling around the porch of Ben's brand-new house that was finished right before winter hit. Gillian just put her house on the market.

Almost everyone on the porch turns their attention to me.

My dad hovers at the top of the porch stairs with a beer in hand. "It started at five," he says in his usual tone of "don't give me excuses, next time get your ass here on time."

"I got held up."

My dad grunts but doesn't give me any more shit. Whoever his random was last night, she must've been good in bed.

I walk right into the house, bypassing everyone, and grab a beer from the fridge. I take a long pull as my eyes scan my brother's place. Pictures of him, Gillian, and Clayton hang on every inch of the walls that aren't covered with sweet sayings regarding family and love and cherishing one another. It's weird—my brother's sweatshirt isn't thrown over the back of the couch, the trash bin is empty, and there are no dishes in the sink. So, this is what it's like when Ben lives with a woman.

"Why are you late?" Ben takes a reprieve from fawning over his woman to bug me.

Moments later, Jude joins us in the kitchen clearly ready to gang up on me with Ben. Not much has changed over the years; they've always been a pain in my ass.

"I had things to do." I tip my beer to my lips again, not really wanting to hash out my problems.

Us Noughton boys are good at hiding our issues. Well, we're good at not sharing them. Neither of them told me when they were about to fuck up their futures with the women they love, but Dad and I knew.

"Things or people?" Jude asks, sliding onto the stool to my right. Why is he getting comfortable? The party is on the porch.

"Already had enough of one flavor?" I quirk an eyebrow, and he throws me that fuck off expression he mastered at the age of six. I hold up my hand. "Thought maybe you needed to use your imagination now that you're chained to Sadie."

"You're an asshole," Jude says, sliding off the stool and heading back to the porch.

"Hold up," Ben says to Jude, and he stops and turns around. Ben looks back at me. "You've been distant. We're trying to make sure things are good with you."

"Winter just ended. My vitamin D level is low."

My excuse is weak. I know it. They both know it. But our dynamic has changed in the past nine months. I'm the odd one out. They have couples' dinners and plan little trips to wineries or to Lincoln for football games. I joined them the first few times, but it gets annoying being the fifth wheel. Not that I'm interested in adding a sixth.

Jude slides back onto the stool. Ben remains standing. Their eyes are still on me.

"Sorry if you guys turned your fun cards in when you hitched your wagons to Gillian and Sadie." I finish my beer.

Their gazes both follow the empty beer bottle I set on the counter. Then they share a look. One that says do you want to call him out, or should I?

I get their protectiveness. I was so young when our mom died. I'm not even sure the vision I remember of her is actually her, and that sucks. I much prefer when they bust my balls than when they act all caring. As if I'm going to throw all the shit that fills my brain daily on their laps.

"I get that the family dynamic has changed." Jude takes the first stab at it, but I put up my hand.

"Listen. I get that you're both in tune with your feelings since you're with the loves of your lives, but there's no need to worry about me. I'm happy being single. I'm not lonely. I love my life."

They glance at one another, and I avoid rolling my eyes. Why do they think they know something I don't? Ben's loved Gillian since high school. Jude's loved Sadie since they were six. Do they see some woman on the periphery of my life while I have my head up my ass like them? No.

Gillian walks inside, their new screen door not banging like the rest of ours because Ben made sure to install a fancy one. It slowly clicks shut when she's halfway into the kitchen.

"Am I interrupting?" She doesn't wait for an answer before opening the oven and pulling out a lasagna.

"I knew I smelled something good." I ignore my brothers and lean over the dish of gooey cheese and sauce. I reach to grab a small piece of burned cheese, and Gillian slaps my hand away. "If a woman could promise me this every night, I'd marry her."

Someone scoffs behind me.

The hairs on my neck rise.

A siren blares in my ears.

My body shifts to fight-or-flight mode.

Briar Adams.

Gillian's half sister who always gives me the cold shoulder, has no end to her snarky comments, and always calls me Little Noughton. Hello, I'm inches taller than my brothers, and there's nothing little about me. Not that she seems to care.

Why does she hate me? I have no fucking clue. I'm not a confrontational kind of guy. I'm easygoing. Everyone loves me. I bring humor into a room. But Briar Adams wouldn't know a joke if she paid an ungodly amount of money to sit in the front row of a packed arena and listen to the hottest comedian.

"Briar," I say with a nod.

The room quiets. Neither of my brothers say a word.

"Ben. Jude. Little Noughton." She nods, standing across the giant kitchen island, glaring at me.

My back straightens as I ready to hash out a few rounds. Then I'll go home to beat off because this woman drives me fucking crazy.

Chapter Four

BRIAR

I didn't plan on coming to the Noughton Sunday dinner. I don't much care for Emmett Noughton. I'm only here because Gillian has been good to me. Ben has been nice. They're all about family and closeness and bonding, which isn't really my thing.

"Hey, Briar." Ben moves in to hug me, but I stiffen, so we awkwardly do a side hug, patting one another on the back.

Thankfully, Jude just raises his hand with a simple, "Hey."

The Noughtons are always welcoming. When I arrived, Bruce wrapped his arms around me, not caring that I drew back. He held me longer than I prefer and squeezed me tightly as if he'd missed me. When he finally released me, he smiled and said he was glad I could make it tonight. Jude's wife, Sadie, who is as sweet as sugar, shifted to get up, but I shooed her back down on account of her swollen belly.

I'm still not completely comfortable with the family dynamic here. It's an enigma I've never solved. I guess that's what happens when your mom runs out on you, and your dad works so much it puts him in an early grave. Sure, I have Koa, my brother, but he's off finding himself somewhere.

"I'm so happy you're home for good." Gillian grabs my hand and pulls me toward the kitchen. Which also means closer to Emmett.

I feel his eyes on me. The way they skirt over my body, and damn it, my body heats, wanting him to look at something he'll never have. I'm wearing my tightest yoga pants and matching sports bra with a sweatshirt unzipped, so it doesn't leave a lot to the imagination, but I was in the middle of practicing my new class set when Gillian called to say the realtor wanted to show the house *immediately.* I'd barely pulled out of the driveway before the realtor showed up with a middle-aged couple.

"I'm sorry you had to leave the house so quickly," Gillian says, stopping me at her giant kitchen island. She tosses a bag of bread on the fancy marble counter. "The realtor said these people want into Willowbrook..." She continues talking as she grabs butter and garlic and all the ingredients for me to make garlic bread. The one recipe my mom perfected and passed on before she ran off.

I glance at Emmett, who is still watching me.

"I'm going to check on Sadie," Jude says and flees the room.

"Yeah, I'll join you." Ben follows his brother. "Emmett?" He nods toward the door that leads to the porch.

Emmett shakes his head but doesn't say anything.

"It's fine, Gill. Thanks for letting me stay there until it sells."

She finally pulls out a bowl and smiles at me. "Are you kidding? You're my sister." She runs her hand down my arm in that loving way a mother might before she turns and grabs salad fixings from the fridge. "Sorry for putting you to work, but you're the best at garlic bread."

"Garlic bread, huh?" Emmett says and pushes himself up

on the counter, watching me intently put the butter in the bowl.

"Don't you have something else to do?" I ask him.

"Emmett, why don't you check if anyone needs refills on their drinks?" Gillian takes a knife to the lettuce.

The sound of the knife hitting the cutting board startles me. I look up to see Gillian's vision only on Emmett.

"I'm not the host, your hubby is."

"He's not my husband," Gillian says, her big diamond ring sparkling under the bright lights over the island.

"Practically." Emmett shrugs. "So, Briar, what brings you back to Willowbrook?"

I cut up the garlic, not looking at him. "The yoga teacher position here on the ranch."

"That's right. I do love downward dog."

"Emmett," Gillian groans. "Ben, come get your brother," she calls.

"Cute. You're one of those," I say, slicing through the garlic faster.

"One of what?" Emmett's interest piques, and I regret engaging him.

"What's up?" Ben walks back in and steals a cucumber from Gillian's cutting board.

"Help Emmett get refills for everyone."

I glance out the corner of my eye to see her give Ben a look and nod in our direction. Gillian already warned me to stay away from Emmett. That he's the last thing I need right now. She has no idea that if Emmett was the last man on this earth, and it was up to us to recreate life, I'd knee him in the balls and push him off a cliff. Okay, that was kind of dramatic.

Emmett leans in close to my ear. "You didn't answer my question."

"Let's go, little brother," Ben says, but Emmett doesn't move.

"Hold up. I'm having a conversation with Briar." Emmett quirks one eyebrow at me.

Why can't he have gained fifty pounds around his middle and grown a few moles on his face? Lost a few teeth? But age has only made Emmett more muscular, more defined. His chin is a goddamn chiseled masterpiece. I bet he could hold me up against a wall and fuck all my problems away.

I still my mind and remind myself I hate the man. "You see yoga as sex positions."

"Emmett!" Ben says louder.

Surprising me, Emmett hops down from the counter. "I just wanted to see that amazing ass of yours up in the air."

"Fucking hell," Ben growls. "Get your ass outside."

Emmett laughs and winks at me before turning toward his brother. "We were discussing her job. You can't blame me for making small talk."

"Small talk my ass."

They walk out to the porch, and through the window, I catch Emmett holding his hands in the air, telling Clayton to throw him the ball.

"I'm sorry. He can be a lot sometimes," Gillian says.

I shake my head at my sweet sister who practically raised me. She really is the best. "I can handle Emmett Noughton."

Then I see him put one hand on the porch railing and jump over it onto the ground below. It's flawless the way his legs swing over and all his weight is held up by one bulging bicep. I need to remember why I hate Emmett. I'm in no place to start anything with any man right now, let alone a man-child like Emmett.

"Well, Ben is going to have a conversation with him." Gillian tosses the salad and sets it aside.

I spread the garlic butter mixture over the bread. She puts it in the oven, then she grabs a wine bottle from the fridge and snatches two glasses. I still for a moment, watching the wine fill the crystal glass. It looks really good, and lord knows I could use it right now to calm my frazzled nerves.

She slides a glass my way, and my shoulders sink. "Tomorrow is my first day, and I don't want to have a headache. Wine always gives me a headache."

Gillian's head tilts, and I prepare for her to push me on the subject. "More for me then. Water's in the fridge." Her phone rings on the counter. "Oh, it's the realtor." She slides her thumb over the screen and walks into the attached living room. Their entire downstairs is open concept. "Hello?"

I check the garlic bread and make a mental note to check it again in a few minutes.

"No way! Are you serious?" Gillian says, her eyes widening in my direction. "Well, yeah, I guess." Her smile dims, and she cringes at me. "No, I see your point. Okay, well..." She stares at me for a long time. "Of course. Yeah. Definitely. I'll take it."

She hangs up and stands in place for a second. That's Gillian though. Always taking a moment to think about her words and what the next step is. She doesn't often act impulsively, and I've always admired that because I'm the opposite. I'm not sure if she was born that way or if it was the years of child-rearing she's done, unable to ever be a child herself.

"Ben!" she calls.

He walks in, looking into the kitchen before finding her in the living room. "What's up?"

"The house is sold. Cash offer, and they want to move in as soon as they can."

And just like that, I'm homeless once again.

Chapter Five

BRIAR

Gillian squeals as Ben picks her up and swings her around the room.

"That's amazing!"

She beams. "I know. I mean, I never thought it'd happen this fast. I figured we'd have it for a while longer."

Gillian's small bungalow in downtown Willowbrook isn't my childhood home. Gillian moved there once Koa and I were old enough to take care of ourselves. After Dad died, she moved us in. Koa had to share a bedroom with Clayton and I had my own. After I went off to school, Koa moved into my old bedroom. It was small but hers.

So while I have no significant attachment to the house, I'm surprised she's so excited. I just drove by my childhood home the other day, remembering the day we moved out after it sold. The feeling of not having anything of my own, a place where I belonged. And here I am in the same situation again. All I have to blame is myself.

Bruce comes in off the porch. "What's going on?"

Ben lowers Gillian's feet to the floor. "Gill sold her house. Cash buyer."

Bruce's eyes widen. A cash buyer is surprising, but maybe the housing market is as crazy here as it was in Chicago. "That's great news."

Everyone else comes in from outside, probably having overheard what's going on. Sadie rushes over and hugs Gillian. Jude nods and gives his congratulations, then Gillian quietly talks to Clayton, and I see him nod a lot. God, she's such a good mom. How did she turn out to be so great when she had no role model?

Bruce turns in my direction and gives me a tight smile.

Oh, fucking hell. I hate that pitying look.

"Shit." Emmett rushes toward me in the kitchen. There's fear in his eyes. His hand lands on my hip, and he shoves me aside.

I stumble, almost falling to the floor, but I catch myself on the edge of the counter. "Excuse me is a word."

"Two actually," he says, snatching the oven mitt off the counter and opening the oven.

A billow of smoke flows from the oven, and my mouth hangs open, watching Emmett take out a tray of burned garlic bread. He sets it next to the lasagna. The bread is black. Great, my first meal after my return, and I ruin the part of dinner I was in charge of.

"Oh no," Gillian says.

A moment later, the smoke alarm rings and everyone scrambles into action. Emmett shuts the oven door, turning off the oven while Ben reaches up to press the button to get the alarm to stop. Gillian grabs a dishcloth and waves the smoke out the screen door while Bruce and Jude open every window that isn't already open.

Sadie is reaching up to turn on the fan when Jude grabs her hips and pulls her away.

"What are you doing?" she asks.

"The baby," he says, turning the fan on himself. "Emmett should've done it."

Emmett scoffs and shakes his head but says nothing.

Ben gets the smoke alarm to stop shrieking, and everyone calms down, but their brand-new house still has a haze of smoke through it.

"I'm so sorry," I say past the lump in my throat.

"It's fine. The excitement." Gillian puts her arm around my shoulders.

"Yeah, ask Emmett about the time he almost burned down our entire house," Jude says.

"I still remember Dad running down in his underwear, swearing and yelling. He picked up Emmett and threw him out of the house." Ben laughs.

"I didn't want him to catch on fire." Bruce shakes his head.

"Sure. That's the reason." Jude and Ben laugh some more.

My gaze goes to Emmett, who isn't laughing. His hands are shoved into his pockets, and he's looking at the floor. The pit in my stomach grows uncomfortably bigger, and I hate that I feel sorry for him.

"You guys were the older brothers. He shouldn't have been cooking anyway," Sadie says.

The three of them banter, but Emmett says nothing.

"The poor guy was just trying to get some attention." Jude swings his arm around Emmett's neck and his knuckles go to his hair.

Emmett squirms out of his hold and pushes Jude away. "Fuck off."

"Want me to go out and get some bread?" I ask, looking for any reason to get out of this uncomfortable situation.

"No, no. We don't need the bread. Come on, guys. Let's eat." Gillian takes the plates over to their giant dining room table and sets them out.

Sadie follows her with the forks and knives.

"I was looking forward to this famous garlic bread." Emmett eyes me, obviously recovered from his brothers' razzing. "All the butter melting down my fingers, me licking it off."

He runs his fingers over his bottom lip, and he gets to me because my mind is now on his fingers. His hands are so big compared to mine, and his fingers are long and thick, and damn it, I wonder what they'd feel like inside me before he licked my juices off them.

"Is everything related to sex for you?" I grab the salad bowl and slide past him.

"I'm not the one who keeps bringing up sex. That's on you." He taps my nose with his finger, then winks again.

"You're so annoying." I turn away from him and take the salad to the table. I hate the fact I didn't have a better comeback. The fact that I'm homeless and just ruined my perfect sister's dinner has me frazzled, plus I'm starting a new job tomorrow.

"Come on. You can do better than that," he whispers in my ear and rounds the table.

I smack my neck where his warm breath hit me as though a mosquito just bit me, when in reality, goose bumps flutter across my flesh.

We all take our seats at the table. Emmett is directly across from me, and I have a feeling he picked that seat on purpose. Why does he get off on trading insults back and forth?

"When will you close?" Bruce asks Gillian once everyone has their lasagna and salads on their plates. No garlic bread, though, thanks to me.

"Brian said probably three weeks or less, since it's a cash offer." She blinks a few times as if she's still surprised.

"And what will you do now, Briar?" Bruce's question throws me.

"She can move in here," Gillian says. "You can have the bedroom next to Clayton's."

I glance at Ben, and he smiles at me, clearly not caring that I'll be imposing. But they've just gotten back together after years apart. They moved in here as a family. Gillian told me about Ben's proposal and how it was all about the three of them starting their new life here. I don't feel right pushing my way into the middle of that, especially with the state of my life.

"I'll just get an apartment." I pick up my water and gulp down a few swigs.

Money will be tight at first, but I'll pick myself up off the floor as I always do.

"Why would you do that? No way. You're staying here." Gillian's eyes dig into mine as if she's trying to see why I'd fight her on this.

Sure, staying at her old house while she was living here was easy and nice, but moving in with them is a whole different story.

"You're welcome here, Briar," Ben says.

I put my fork down and wipe my mouth with the cloth napkin. "Thank you, but I just..." Everyone's eyes are on me, and I shift in the wooden chair. "I'll be fine in an apartment."

"Not when we have all this room here." Bruce leans back in his seat, staring at me. "You're family. Don't waste money on an apartment."

"What about the girls' house?" Sadie says.

"That could work," Jude says and looks at me. "Our female cousins have their own house."

"But there's only four bedrooms," Bruce says, shaking his head.

"Really. I'll be fine," I say.

"You could move in with us," Sadie says, but Jude's side-eyes her.

"I'm sure she doesn't want to hear you banging all night."

Emmett leans back with his beer in hand. He tilts his head with a smirk as if I owe him one for getting me out of that jam.

"Why don't you want to move in here?" Gillian asks with hurt in her voice.

"I know what we'll do," Bruce interrupts. Thank goodness. All the attention around the table shifts to Bruce, who bears a wide smile. "You'll move in with Emmett."

Oh no, he didn't. I must have heard him wrong. "I'm sorry?"

"Emmett. He's got that big house, and it's only him." Bruce looks around as though he's Newton and just discovered gravity.

"He doesn't even shit there," Ben says, and Gillian elbows him.

"Oh, I'm fine." I give Bruce a wan smile, not daring to look Emmett's way.

"You're practically brother and sister now," Jude says, laughing right after as though he's been waiting to get that out this whole dinner.

"Stop it, both of you," Bruce says with a stern voice. "You let us know when you need your stuff moved and Emmett will get you situated at his place." He picks up his fork and piles a heaping bite of lasagna into his mouth, not seeming to notice everyone trading glances over the table. "I'm glad that's settled."

They can't be serious. Surely they don't expect me to move in with Emmett. As if my life isn't upside down enough right now, it somehow got worse.

Chapter Six

EMMETT

I'm a gentleman. People don't think I am, but I am. I was raised to be one. As much as I'm an asshole, I give a shit about people and their feelings.

Clearly, something is going on with Briar. She's not giving me the attitude that she usually does. And I'm annoyed because I get off on her snarky comments.

Again, I love my family, but how can they seriously not have a clue why she doesn't want to live with them? Why would she want to live with any couple who just got together?

So I don't say a word about my dad's decision. Because that's what it is. He thinks his idea is brilliant—though when Gillian first announced that she'd sold the house, I thought about where Briar would go and how she could stay at my house. There are three empty bedrooms down the hall from mine. Not that I want her to live with me. Of course I don't.

But now that my dad has decided it, it's going to happen. We might all be fucking adults, but that doesn't change the fact that when my dad wants something done, it's easier to do it. Gillian must realize this too because she doesn't fight him on his idea.

Briar goes to the bathroom after dinner, and I take the opportunity to go out on the porch with my dad. I need to figure out a way for him to think it's his idea that Briar moving in with me won't work.

"Dad," I whisper. "I'm not sure Briar wants to live with me."

"Why would that be?" He stares at the pond, watching the ducks flying low until they splash into the water.

"First off, she hates me. Like loathes me." I really wish I knew why, but what do I care? It's her problem.

"All the better then."

I glance over my shoulder. Ben, Clayton, and Jude are doing the dishes while Gillian and Sadie gossip at the dining room table and set up the games. God help me. Briar must still be in the bathroom.

"Why would it be better that she hates me?" Sometimes I think my dad talks in code.

"She won't be tempted to sleep with you."

I scoff and draw back. "What?"

Dad looks at me. "You're a younger version of me. Hard for women to resist. Plus, and don't tell your brothers..." His eyes follow their laughter inside until he looks back at me. "You have my charm. But it seems like Briar needs her people right now. She needs family and to feel loved."

"You should have your own show, Dr. Bruce."

He shoots me a look that says cut the shit. "She's back in Willowbrook because she doesn't have anywhere else to go."

"Why would you say that? Did she tell you that?"

Sometimes people do tell my dad a lot of shit they don't tell others. Five years after Ben left, I woke up to find Gillian at our kitchen table in tears, talking to my dad. Sadie was just having coffee with him the other day, talking about becoming a new parent.

"I've seen a lot of people come back to town throughout

my life. There are only a few reasons why they come back after leaving it in the first place. More often than not, they have nowhere else to go. It's important we keep her on the ranch, make her feel like she's a part of our family. She hasn't had the easiest road."

Neither have I, but I don't say that. Sure, I lost my mom, but I had my dad and brothers, plus all my cousins, aunts, and uncles. From the little I know about Briar, which is practically nothing other than that she's Gillian's half sister, I don't think she's had much of a support system beyond her sister and brother.

"She might not last long. Doesn't exactly seem to be comfortable here." I stuff my hands in my pockets, watching Briar through the window. She sits down next to Gillian, who places her hand on Briar's forearm.

Dad laughs. "I wouldn't worry about that. Let's go do game night."

"Wait, what do you mean?" I ask before he can open the screen door.

He looks perplexed. "I'm sure the two of you can manage in that large house of yours without killing one another."

"I'm not so sure," I mumble.

He walks into the house, and I stare at the lake for a moment before joining them, which I regret immediately when I see the pair-ups.

Ben is next to Gillian.

Jude has his arm around Sadie.

Dad and Clayton are in hushed whispers.

And Briar is sitting by herself, her arms crossed, her eyes boring into mine. Fucking hell.

I guess the new Noughton duo starts now.

"COME ON." I HIT THE PAPER OVER AND OVER AGAIN with the marker while the sand slowly disappears through the hourglass.

"A guy. I said a guy," Briar says, leaning back in her chair, her arms still crossed.

"Same thing, different word." My eyes narrow on her.

"You can't talk," Gillian says.

I look at her. "Thank you, Pictionary Police."

"Hey," Ben chimes in, and I give him my palm.

"Okay, how about this," I say and draw a house.

"Man of the house?" Briar says in a bored tone.

I get it, I don't want to be here either, but here we are. Does she have no competitive streak? She has to want to win.

I shake my head and draw an arrow from the man to the house.

"Man in the house?"

I growl and draw a gingerbread woman in a dress.

"Married couple? Love?" She shows no excitement or urgency that we're about to lose this round.

Finally, I draw a dick between the gingerbread's legs and circle it.

"The size of your dick?"

"Briar." Gillian eyes Clayton.

"Please, Gill, he knows what a dick is." Briar rolls her eyes.

I love that she didn't apologize.

"Still." Gillian sits back. Hopefully, that will shut her up for a bit about the rules.

I circle the entire man and point at the dick between his legs.

"I got nothing," Briar says.

I stare at the ceiling and finally decide to draw an oven and a cookie sheet with all the little men on it, minus the dicks, in the hopes she'll get it. I turn away from the paper, and she stares at it. My eyes zero in on the sand slipping through the small hole.

"Ohhh. You went about it entirely the wrong way. Why didn't you do that in the beginning instead of drawing the house and giving him a dick? I told you, you only think about sex."

"Say the damn word," I grind out between my teeth.

"Gingerbread man," she says nonchalantly right before the last grain of sand slips to the bottom of the hourglass.

"Jesus, that was like pulling teeth." I put the cap on the marker and set it down.

"You guys are finally on the board." Sadie claps and places a slash next to our names.

Every other team has cute names—Billian and Judie and Bro Crew. But when it came time for us to give our team a name, we just said Emmett and Briar. We fought about whose name went first, and eventually Sadie said she'd write them alphabetically. I've never wished more that I was named Bennett like my cousin.

Everyone at the table disperses to take a short break, some going to the bathroom, others getting drinks, and it leaves Briar and me by ourselves. How wonderful.

"You just like things to be dramatic," she says when I sit next to her.

"Are you kidding me? You almost gave me a heart attack." I down the rest of my beer.

"It's a game. Grow up."

"A game? It's Pictionary against my brothers. It's more than a game." I'll switch to water now since I'm working early in the morning.

"I hate competitive guys." She rolls her eyes and finally moves from her stoic position and grabs her own water.

"Good, that means you won't be sneaking into my bed in the middle of the night."

"You wish."

Fuck, do I, but the hell if she'll ever know that. "You'd be so lucky."

Her face crinkles into a disgusted expression. "Ew... no walking around naked, okay? I don't need to see that thing." Her gaze falls to my crotch, and damn if it doesn't twitch. "It would ruin my day."

"Let's remember that *you're* moving in with *me*. It's my house, and if I want to be naked, I will be."

"Fine, then I will too," she says as though that would be a threat.

"I knew you wanted me to see your titties." I down the cold water, hoping like hell it cools down my body while I'm thinking of stripping off that sports bra and seeing her tits. I wouldn't mind...

Fuck that. Stop.

"You're so full of yourself."

I grin at her. "Most women like my confidence."

Briar stares at me long and hard, back to her cool demeanor. "You better hide the knives."

My head falls back in laughter, but when I straighten, she's staring at me. Not even one of her perfectly arched eyebrows is raised.

"Fuck, you scare me," I say, not realizing until she cracks a small smile that I said that aloud.

Now I just gave the enemy intel.

I leave her alone at the table before I give her any more incriminating truths. Like how I want to fuck her so badly, my cock aches.

Chapter Seven

BRIAR

I walk into The Getaway Lodge, and Ben's Aunt Darla stands up from a plush chair in the sitting area. It's nestled beside another chair, near a large sofa in front of a fireplace that isn't currently on. The Getaway Lodge is cozy and welcoming with light-colored walls and dark floors.

"Briar." She already has her arms open wide on her way over to me.

What's with this family and hugging?

But she's my new boss, so I let her envelop me in a hug and squeeze me so tightly I fear I'll break. "Hi, Mrs. Owens."

She pulls back but holds me by my upper arms. "Oh no, you don't. I'm Darla."

I smile. "Okay."

"No, say it," she says, lightly squeezing my arms. "Come on now."

"Darla. Thanks for giving me this opportunity."

She releases me, and the anxiety catapulting inside me lessens until she pulls me into her chest again.

She's gorgeous, with dark hair and green eyes that hold so much warmth and love.

"We're so happy to have you." She finally stops hugging me and keeps her hands to herself. "Come on, let's go see Jensen in the kitchen. Did you eat this morning?"

"I had a smoothie," I say. It's the truth, but in reality, I was only able to swallow a few mouthfuls before I started to feel sick.

"A smoothie?" She tsks. "You kids. You need more than that to sustain your day."

I follow her through the building, past a set of curious eyes from behind the front desk.

"No wonder there's nothing to you. I wish I could offer you a few of my pounds, but Mr. Owens..." She stops before a swinging door and eyes me. "Brad to you. He likes me with a little extra to hold on to." She laughs and walks through the door.

The kitchen is amazing, and I'd never guess it was attached to a lodge. Stainless steel is everywhere, and there are a few people walking around, each one in a white coat.

"Jensen!" Darla hollers and weaves through the chaos that looks like the breakfast rush. She pats one guy on the back as she passes. "Good morning, Hayes."

"Mornin', Darla." The blond-haired guy smiles, and his eyes linger on me for a beat before he goes back to his station.

I hate being the newbie.

"Grandma!" A little girl runs over, and Darla opens her arms wide to receive her. She's cute with dirty-blonde hair in braids, although they're slightly crooked in the back, with a zigzag part down the middle.

"Wren, what are you doing in the kitchen?" Darla asks.

"Wren!" a man shouts into the kitchen.

"I'm sorry, did everyone forget that this is my workspace?" a guy wiping down the edges of the plates says.

"She saw Mom and got away from me." The man who yelled for the little girl stops when he sees me. "Briar Adams?"

"Yep, she's all grown up." Darla picks up the little girl, and her long legs swing over her grandma's hips.

"Hi, Bennett," I say. "And Wren." I put my hand out to the little girl.

Gillian practically gave me a quiz on who's who on the ranch. Although I went to high school with all of them, they're all older than me, so I wasn't sure they'd remember me.

"You have pretty hair," the little girl says.

"So do you."

"Daddy can't do my hair." Her eyes fixate on my side braid that was about all I could manage this morning.

"If you'd sit still." Bennett shakes his head at me and smiles.

If I have my math right, Bennett is the same age as Emmett. People always asked why their moms would give them names that sound the same when they're so close in age and cousins.

"He can't even do a ponytail. Will you do my hair?" Wren tugs one of her ponytail holders off the end of her braid.

"Wren, you have school," Bennett says.

"I'm sorry, but I have to start my job." I give her an exaggerated frown.

Darla lowers Wren to the floor. "You're fine. Sit down at the table." Darla points at a table that's off to the side. "I'll grab a hairbrush." Darla turns to leave the room.

"No, you won't, Aunt Darla. This is a kitchen. You will not be combing hair, or braiding hair, or whatever." Jenson comes over and greets me with a hug. Another damn hug. "Hey, Briar, welcome. Good to see you."

"Thanks, Jenson. You too."

"You're such a stickler." Darla rolls her eyes. "You need to make Briar something to eat. She only had a smoothie this morning."

Jenson stares down at me. He's tall just like Emmett. "Are you hungry?"

I shake my head.

"She will be in an hour," Darla says.

"Stop shoving food down people's throats, Mom." Bennett puts his hand on Wren's shoulders. "Let's go back into the dining room. Your pancakes are probably cold."

Wren crosses her arms. "Not unless she comes to do my braid like hers."

Bennett glares at his daughter.

Darla laughs. "Hey, it's payback for all the grief you gave me when you were her age. You and Emmett gave me anxiety with all your antics."

I stand in the kitchen, unsure what I should do. I thought I was here to lead yoga classes, but at this point, it seems I'm supposed to braid a little girl's hair and eat breakfast.

"Why don't you head into the dining room? I can make you some eggs. How do you want them?" Jensen steps back over to the work area.

"Um..." Just the thought of eggs makes me want to vomit.

"I get it, but honestly, it's better to make Aunt Darla think you're listening to her." He smirks.

Jensen is kind of cute in that clean-cut way. Maybe it's his chef jacket and meticulous kitchen that makes me think of him as a guy who likes everything neat and orderly. Unfortunately, for some damn reason, I always want the bad boy.

"Oh, look who's starting today."

I close my eyes at Emmett's voice behind me. Jensen laughs.

"Scrambled is fine," I say.

Jenson nods. "Get out of my kitchen, Emmett." He points at the door and directs orders to his staff.

Okay, there's definitely something hot about watching him do that.

"Sorry, he's off-limits," Emmett says, his voice closer now, then I feel the heat of his body behind me.

"Whatever." I circle around, managing to sneak by him and out the door, then I turn right to find the dining room.

Darla has Wren in her lap, braiding her hair while Bennett eats a plate of pancakes that I think must have been Wren's since chocolate chips and whipped cream cover them. Then again, maybe he's a man-child like Emmett.

"What's up, Danson?" Emmett smacks his cousin on the shoulder and flips the chair around so he's straddling it. Neanderthal.

"Come sit." Darla pats the chair next to her.

I take the seat across from Emmett, who's picked up a stray fork and is cutting into the pancakes Bennett is eating. I'm not sure why Emmett referred to him as Danson when he sat down.

"Grandma!" Wren moves forward, and her hair slips from Darla's fingers.

This is the weirdest day of my life. I thought they'd show me the studio. I'd tell them my plans for the classes. They'd tell me my schedule. But instead, I'm being forced to eat eggs, and Wren is pleading with the brightest blue eyes, silently asking if she can come over to my lap. Meanwhile, Emmett is one step away from eating with his hands. Maybe I should've stayed in Chicago.

"I can do your hair," I say because who doesn't want to butter up their boss?

"Yay!" Wren slides off Darla's lap.

Darla happily hands me the ponytail holders and brush. Thankfully, we're tucked into a corner. I wonder if this is the family table.

Wren hops up on my lap. She barely weighs anything.

Emmett finishes chewing and watches me brush her hair.

I'd ask him what he finds so interesting about it, but I don't really care to know what's going on in his head.

"Did y'all hear Briar is moving in with me?" He grabs Bennett's coffee just as Bennett reaches for it and swallows it down.

"Oh really?" Bennett asks, eyeing me.

"You're so lucky." Wren's shoulders slump.

I raise my eyebrows.

Bennett fills me in. "Wren loves Emmett's no rules policy."

"I have rules. Right, Wren?" He winks at her. The same wink he gives me all the time, and I shouldn't be upset that it isn't reserved for me. That's just Emmett.

Wren giggles like all the high school girls used to when we were in school together. Although, I was a freshman when he was a senior. Is there any woman besides me he can't wrap around his finger?

"I heard something about this earlier today. Gillian called and asked me about the girls' house and whether there was a spare room she didn't know about." Darla pours herself more coffee from the carafe.

It feels as if I'm never getting out of this room.

Emmett scoffs and leans back in his chair. "She's so worried about me wanting to f—"

"Emmett!" Bennett scolds.

Darla gives him the evil eye.

"If you'd let me finish, I was saying she's worried I'll do funny pranks on Briar."

Wren laughs. "Like that time you put pepper in Uncle Jude's drink, and he threw up?" She turns to look back at me, and I almost lose my grip on her hair. "It was so funny."

Emmett puts up his hand to high-five her. "Couldn't have done it without my accomplice." He lets her smack his large palm with her small one.

"Yeah, that was great, having to put a flashlight against my glass for two weeks to make sure nothing extra was added." Bennett stares at Emmett with zero expression on his face.

"Emmett does know how to be a juvenile," I say.

Bennett snickers and wipes his mouth, then grabs Wren's jacket from the back of his chair. "We have to get going."

"Almost finished." I secure the end of her braid with the ponytail holder. "All set."

Wren's little fingers run over the braid. "Do I look just like you?"

"You look beautiful," I say.

"Am I as pretty as Briar, Emmett?" She turns to him as Bennett slides her arms into her jacket and grabs her backpack.

A flick of annoyance lands on Emmett's face for a moment, but he forces a smile. "Prettier," he says, a conniving smirk taking residence on his lips.

Wren beams at his compliment and waves goodbye to us as her dad ushers her out the door.

"Don't you need to go to work or something?" I ask as my eggs are placed in front of me.

"I'm working in a horse so my appetite is bigger than ever."

The waitress who slid my plate in front of me places a huge plate of food in front of Emmett. Eggs, bacon, ham, biscuits, and gravy. Then she brings over a huge waffle. My stomach rumbles with nausea at the thought of him consuming that. Not because it doesn't look delicious, but because I can only imagine how sick I'd feel if I ate it all.

Darla's phone rings. "Excuse me a sec." She gets up from the table and walks away.

"And once again, it's just the two of us." He smiles.

I cross my legs and kick him under the table. "Peachy."

I take my fork to down the eggs. Maybe if I finish them, then I can start my job.

Darla comes back in. "I'm so sorry, we have an emergency

at The Harvest Depot. Emmett, be a good boy and show Briar to the studio. I'll be back as soon as I can."

This has to be a joke.

"She didn't say you were going to death row. The majority of women would love to spend time with me," Emmett says.

I don't say anything.

"They never want to leave my bed."

"After you make them breakfast in the morning, of course." I pour myself an orange juice from the carafe on the table.

"Cute that you think I'd serve them breakfast. They're gone before dawn, darlin'."

"Spare me the details." I sip my orange juice.

"Hurry up, and maybe we can do some happy baby stretches together."

I groan and bury my head in my plate, hoping his big plate of food will keep him from talking anymore. "Doing research on yoga positions?"

"I plan on taking a class." He winks before burying his face in his food, devouring the biscuits and gravy.

This cannot be my new normal. I have to figure out a way out of this.

Chapter Eight

EMMETT

I'm in the horse barn, shoeing all the damn horses because supposedly I'm the best at it. The horses are calmer when I do it. That's what Jude and my dad say. It's bullshit. I bitch about it, but I don't mind. I kind of like when it's just the horses and me. I play my country music, focus on my task, and it clears my head. Gives me a sense of accomplishment when I'm done taking the old shoes off, getting the hooves filed down, fitting them for their new shoes, and nailing them in. Sometimes it's nice to be alone with my thoughts.

I hear rustling behind me and groan. Someone is gonna bother me, and it better not be fucking Jude. He's been up my ass all week. Funny how he never wanted to show me shit until he got with his childhood best friend, and now they're expecting a baby. Now he wants to dump everything on me, right when I come up with a plan I know would kill it here.

I keep working to fit the horseshoes for my dad's horse, Legend. I always save Brutus for last because he's mine.

"There you are." Ben walks in. He's dressed in track pants and a sweatshirt. He coaches the high school football team, but they're not playing right now, so he decided to take on the track team as well. None of us Noughton boys are ones to sit around and do nothing.

"Where else would I be?" I go to the forge and put the horseshoe in to heat up the metal so I can mold it as perfectly as I can.

"I was looking for you." He pets Magnum, running his hand down his mane.

"Well, you found me." I keep working.

"I heard you showed Briar the studio yesterday. That you showed up at breakfast." He grabs a brush and brushes Magnum.

Ben doesn't work on the farm. Magnum is the only part of him down here. Even when he was younger, Ben never had to work the ranch much because he was so focused on football. Sure, during harvest and planting season, he helped. We needed as many hands as we could get. But since our family farm got bigger and started making a bigger profit while he was away playing professional football, he doesn't know much about what goes on around here.

"What's your point?" I peek up at him before banging the horseshoe into the right shape.

"Why were you there?"

I take the aggression running through my veins and try to cool it by dousing the horseshoe in the bucket of cold water, imagining it's my temper. The water splashes over the edge, and I continue to swish the shoe around, not wanting to have this conversation with him.

"Did Gillian send you?" I ask.

"No." He puts down the brush and walks back out of Magnum's stall, then sits on the bench in front of me, resting his forearms on his thighs. "But she is worried."

"She has nothing to worry about." I keep my head down because my brothers can call out my bullshit just as well as I can theirs.

"I've seen you look at her, Emmett."

Ben and I have never really fought. That was always more him and Jude, but I can feel an argument brewing between us.

"I'm not blind." I place the horseshoe on Legend and hammer it into his hoof, careful not to hurt him. "Just spit it out."

"I don't know the details, but something bad happened in Chicago. Briar's hurting, and she needs this time to recharge."

"And?" I move to Legend's next hoof to start the process over again.

"She's vulnerable. And we both know you're only interested in sex."

I glance up at him through my eyelashes. "I told you that you don't have anything to worry about."

"I want insurance on that."

I gently place Legend's hoof back on the ground and stand up straight. "I think you're forgetting that Briar is a big girl. Last I checked, she can make her own mistakes."

His eyebrows rise at the word mistake.

"Not like she'd regret being with me."

His eyebrows draw down, and his shoulders fall. "Cut the shit, Emmett. I'm here to make it worth your while not to lay a finger on Briar."

I step closer, crossing my arms. "Do tell."

He rises to his feet, but I've still got inches on him. The day my pencil mark on the wall was higher than his and Jude's was one of the best in my life. It's the little things, but being taller than my older brothers and seeing the irritation on their faces was epic in my world.

"You'll have my vote."

I tilt my head. "Excuse me?"

He runs his fingers through his hair. "You heard me. The dude ranch thing you want to do. You have my vote if you keep away from Briar."

Dad, Aunt Darla, and Aunt Bette became the owners of our farm after our grandparents died. Now, over the years, all the kids have been given their slice of the pie, so to get this dude ranch approved, I need at least eight votes, including mine. Ben is a huge vote, but he's the only one whose steady paycheck doesn't rely on the ranch. Like, be real—he has enough money from his football career that he doesn't have to work another day in his life if he doesn't want to. Of course, Dad would never allow him to sit around all day.

"Let me be sure I've got this right—you're going to give me your vote in exchange for me not touching Briar?"

Ben looks as though he's signing his life away, but he nods.

I click my tongue off the roof of my mouth. "One vote doesn't make it happen."

He sighs.

It's an easy deal to make since there's a lot against me when it comes to Briar. She hates me for one, and I doubt she'd ever entertain any type of arrangement between us, although I do catch her checking me out occasionally. Second, I made myself a deal a long time ago never to fuck anyone my cousins or family members are friends with, which was more a lesson learned than something I came up with on my own.

So I can play this multiple ways, but there's only one way that assures me Ben will not only vote for my idea but go to bat for me with my cousins. We have a big family meeting in two months to discuss what's working, what's not, and what we can do to improve the ranch. I plan on announcing my idea after I film a few more things on the ranch and see how many views I can get. Today, I was going to film myself putting new horseshoes on Brutus.

"I don't know, Ben. I mean, I feel this pull to her."

He growls. Literally, an animalistic sound rumbles up from his throat. "Don't play games."

I laugh because it's comical how protective my brothers

are about anything that affects their women. I mean, can regular pussy really be that good?

"Help me get the votes I need, and it's a deal. I won't lay a finger on little Briar."

"Good." He holds his palm out to me.

"You better campaign for this idea like you're really behind it and not say some bullshit like 'I told Emmett if he didn't go after Briar, then I'd help him get the votes.' I want real excitement."

He nods. "Fine."

"And Gilly Bean can't know."

His eyes narrow. "I'm not lying to her."

"I'm not asking you to lie. I'm telling you to keep it between us. She's not going to pry if I'm holding up my end of the bargain."

He spits again on his hand. "Fine. Now fucking shake on it."

"Say please," I say, delaying because I realize that maybe I should be offended by this whole arrangement. Am I really that bad of a choice for Briar that he's willing to do this? I may have my fun, but I'm not into dicking girls around and hurting them.

I shake my head to free all the insecurities inflicted on me by being the youngest, most "immature" brother, which is a role I play like a damn Oscar-award winner. They want it, they expect it, and I give it to them on a silver platter.

"Shake my damn hand," Ben says, low and growly again.

I spit in my palm and shake hands with him. Why did we ever think that sharing saliva made our promises to one another more binding? Kids are stupid, and apparently, we still are since we're continuing the tradition.

"Who do you want me to hit up first?" Ben grabs a towel off the bench and wipes his hand.

"The girls."

He groans, but I need the girls if I'm going to get eight votes. "Fine."

"Good doing business with you. Now get the fuck out of here so I can finish this job. You'll be happy to know that I have a date tonight."

"With your hand?" Ben asks, already walking backward out of the barn.

"With Briar."

His face falls.

"I'm kidding," I say. "I've never lost a bet, and I won't lose this one."

He nods a few times, but his expression says he's unsure.

I could do this in my sleep. I should draw up the plans for the dude ranch right now. This is a bet I'm gonna win, hands down.

Chapter Nine

BRIAR

Today is my first official day of running a yoga class in Willowbrook. Since The Getaway Lodge isn't huge, and there aren't a huge number of guests at any one time, they've allowed people who aren't guests at the lodge to pay to join the class. I'm really not sure how many people will come, and I worry this job will be extinct before I can make some money. Then I'm not sure what I'll do. Gillian mentioned I could take her hours at her best friend Laurel's bakery since she's so busy now, but it's not that many hours. Certainly not enough to live on.

As usual, Darla's hip is propped up against a chair as she talks more with her hands than her voice to a guest. She spots me and excuses herself with a touch of her hand on the person's shoulder. Darla has a grace I'm not sure I could master even if I went to finishing school. She's welcoming and sweet and kind, but she doesn't have to force it. It's just who she is. Whereas I always come off as abrupt and even cold, sometimes unintentionally.

"Briar, you always look so put together." She takes my

wrists and brings me to her before wrapping her arms around me and hugging me just as tightly as she did the first time.

I pat her back, but it looks awkward to spectators, I'm sure. While she's totally put together, my hair is thrown up in a messy bun, and I'm dressed in matching yoga pants and a sports bra. "Thanks, Darla."

She pulls away but doesn't release me, as if her hands have to be on some part of my body. It's nurturing, and other than Gillian, no woman in my life has ever been like this with me.

"Did you eat?" She asks the question, but I'm pretty sure she knows the answer.

I should be able to tell a little white lie and say yes, but something about Darla makes the lie unable to come out. "No. But I have a protein bar in my bag."

She scoffs and rolls her eyes. "You kids. A protein bar isn't going to give you the energy you need."

Her hand falls to mine, and she escorts me to the family table.

Bennett and Wren are already seated, her hair in a ponytail off to one side that doesn't look as though it was done on purpose. Wren looks up from her pancakes, and her eyes widen. The fork drops to the table, then to the floor. Bennett bends down to get it, calling her name. But Wren is weaving through the tables, her eyes growing wider with every step.

"Oh, she sees someone she likes," Darla says and releases me.

Wren rushes over, and her cute pink Converses skid to a stop in front of me. The infectious smile drops, and her chin dips down.

"What's wrong?" I ask.

"You didn't open your arms." She crosses her small arms over her body.

I'm not great with kids. I've never really been around them, and I swear they can feel my anxiety.

"Oh, I'm sorry." I frown.

Her attention drifts behind me, and she runs around me. "Emmett!"

I glance over my shoulder to see her in his arms and decide to eat quickly so I can move on. I'm not sure why he's here. I thought farm work was an all-day thing.

"She didn't put out her arms," Wren complains to him.

"Maybe she didn't know you like that," Emmett says.

"Well, I do." I hear Wren huff.

"Then tell her."

I ignore that they're talking about me because I'm not a confrontational person, especially with a six-year-old.

"Good morning, Briar," Bennett says before shoveling the last of his food into his mouth.

"You're going to be late," Darla says.

Bennett gives her a look like no shit, dropping his fork, then wipes his mouth and swipes Wren's jacket from the back of her chair.

"Miss Briar?"

I look to my right and see Wren standing next to the table with her hands clasped together in front of her. I turn in my seat. "Yes, Wren?"

She glances at Emmett and back at me. A huge breath falls out of her as if she's summoning the courage to say what she needs to say. I so get her.

"I was really excited to see you, and I like it when... um..." Again, her eyes shift to Emmett, and this time, I let mine move in his direction as well. He nods at Wren. "I like to run into people's arms."

"Thatta girl," Emmett says, and I hate the way the warmth in his voice melts my heart a little. He's teaching her to speak up for herself, even for a little thing like this.

I slide my chair around so that I'm facing her. "I'm sorry.

I've never really been around kids before, so I don't know how to react."

I hate that Emmett is hearing me expose my vulnerability.

"When I run, you hold your arms out." She says it matter-of-factly.

"Wren, you can't make people do what you want," Bennett says from behind me.

"Danson, she's speaking her truth, saying what's important to her," Emmett says. I still don't know why he's always calling Bennett Danson. I wasn't in their crowd back in high school, but I'm sure it's a nickname. "You'll want her to have that when she starts dating."

"Dating? Are you trying to give me a heart attack?" Bennett walks around me and slides the jacket on Wren with her help.

"Okay, next time you see me, I'll open my arms," I say. "Now turn around real quick."

She does as she's told, and I feel all their eyes on me as I take out her haphazard ponytail and fix it so it's in the middle of her head.

"Love your shoes, by the way," I say once I'm done.

"That was good. Complimenting me," Wren says. "She's a good one." She looks at Emmett.

He shakes his head, sitting down and stealing what I think is Wren's plate of food that isn't quite finished. He shrugs. "She's a woman. They live for compliments."

I narrow my eyes at him.

"Gotta go. Last goodbyes." Bennett grabs her backpack from Emmett since he took over Wren's seat.

Wren goes around the table and hugs everyone, including me. "And I like hugs goodbye. It's a security thing."

Bennett glances at Darla, and she frowns. I'm missing something there. I hug Wren, but not nearly as tight as Darla.

"I should get to the studio and set up." I move to climb out of the chair to make my escape.

"You need to eat properly," Darla says, lifting her coffee mug. There's nothing in front of her to eat. Maybe she already did.

"How do you expect to stay in shape and be limber without the proper nutrients?" Emmett asks, finishing off what looks like french toast with strawberries. If I was comfortable, I might cut a piece off for myself, it looks so good.

"Why are you here?" I ask, stripping my eyes away from his french toast that's dripping with syrup. I've never wanted a sugary breakfast more in my life.

"It's my break time."

"He stops by to see Wren. They have a close relationship." Darla is clearly telling me the truth.

I can't help but wonder why Emmett was trying to hide it. His relationship with Wren is endearing. Could there be a soft heart under that jokester exterior?

"That's nice." I shift again to flee the room.

"I'm letting you get away with it this time, but tomorrow, you eat. I'll have Jensen prepare something for you."

"She's eye-fucking my french toast, so maybe that's a good choice." Emmett lifts his fork with a strawberry and french toast, syrup streaming down it, toward me. "I promise I don't have cooties."

I roll my eyes.

Darla laughs.

"No, thanks."

He slides the fork into his mouth, his eyes shutting for a moment as I'm sure the sweetness from the strawberry and syrup mix together to explode on his taste buds. His expression shifts to pure enjoyment, and I find myself jealous as hell. Damn him.

"I gotta go." I stand from the chair.

Darla waves goodbye, watching me with her coffee mug poised in front of her mouth. She has a smile I can't decipher, but I choose to let it go and focus on getting to the studio.

On the way there, my stomach clenches, and I curl in on myself for a moment. I grab the edge of a door frame to steady myself, taking long, slow breaths until the nausea retreats. It always hits at the worst and most unexpected times.

"Boo," Emmett whispers in my ear.

I remove my hand from my stomach. Nauseated or not, I need to escape him. "Don't you have to work?"

"I told you I was on my break, but I'm actually here on business."

I continue walking through the lodge to the studio they set up for me, which I think used to be a small party room. I'm assuming it hasn't been used since they built The Knotted Barn, where all the wedding receptions happen now.

"What kind of business would you have with me?"

"I heard a rumor that you're moving in with the girls."

How does he know? I only heard last night when Gillian came over to her old house to pack up the basement and said that she'd arranged for me to stay with the girls, so I don't have to live with Emmett.

Gillian has done a lot of kind and unselfish things for me in my lifetime, and I appreciate her active approach, but if she's worried I can't control myself around Emmett, she needn't bother. As if just because the man is tall and built and has that playboy persona I love, I can't keep my pussy under lock and key. But really, she's probably doing me a favor because though I won't fuck him, I might go to jail if I have to live with Emmett.

"So I'm told."

"Good. I didn't want you at my house anyway."

I stop in the doorway to the studio and look at him.

He laughs. "I'm kidding, but you'll be much happier there. But please don't sync to their schedule. There's one week every month when all of them have their periods. I've marked it in my calendar, so I know to be on my best behavior."

He's got to be joking, but I don't say anything. I just stare at him, unimpressed.

"I'm kidding. You really don't get my humor, huh? Isn't that a thing, though? All the women synching to the same schedule?"

"I guess," I answer, not really wanting to talk about this.

A line of women are coming down the hall with yoga mats swung over their shoulders. They're all talking loudly, and some hold coffees or drinks from the café in the lobby of the lodge. There are a lot more women than I thought would be here, which is job security, but still, my nerves pile up.

The nausea reappears. Maybe I should have eaten.

"Excuse me," I say and run to the bathroom down the hall.

I push open the door and fall to my knees in front of a toilet without shutting the stall door. I'm unsure how I have anything inside me because I have barely had an appetite lately.

Mindlessly, I press down the lever on the toilet and tilt my head back with my eyes closed, taking deep breaths in hopes of calming my hormones.

"Are you okay?"

Shit. I turn around, and there's Emmett leaning into the stall with his hands anchored to the stall frame.

"This is a woman's bathroom." I quickly get to my feet, wiping my mouth with the back of my hand.

"Not my first time."

"Spare me your kiss-and-tell stories." I wash my hands before taking a paper towel to dry them and run across my mouth.

"Why are you throwing up?" he asks, disregarding my jab.

"Must be something I ate." I walk by him, but he lightly clasps my elbow in his large hand.

"You're pregnant." He says it with certainty.

I have no idea how he'd know or guess. The man knows nothing about me.

"What? Why would you think that?" I act as if he's the kid at the board in class who can't solve the problem, all while he solved it before it was even a question.

"You are," he says, so self-assured.

I momentarily go on the defense, ready to cut him to shreds, but there's no comeback in my head. Damn pregnancy brain. "You don't know what you're talking about."

I yank my elbow away and walk out of the bathroom, running smack dab into Gillian wearing a cute yoga outfit with a new mat swung over her shoulder.

She looks at Emmett and me, who's followed me out, and frowns. "What exactly is going on?"

Oh hell, how did my life get even more complicated by returning to Willowbrook?

Chapter Ten

BRIAR

You'd think Gillian just found me in the bathroom with my professor or therapist or something. Emmett is her fiancé's brother. Even if we had been making out or something, it wouldn't be forbidden or wrong. And where is her trust in me?

"Nothing," I say, walking by her and into the studio.

"Emmett!" There's censure in her voice.

I turn at the entrance and return to her because Emmett didn't do anything wrong. Sure, it's weird that he followed me into the bathroom, but if it was really to make sure I was okay, can I fault that decision? No.

"Nothing happened, Gill."

Emmett holds up his hands. "Hey, I'm sure if I would've tried anything, I'd be bent over in pain right now."

"And he's not." I wave my hand up and down his body to show he's perfectly fine.

Emmett gives me a look, shifting his gaze from Gillian to me. Is he asking me if she knows? He doesn't even know. I never confirmed it for him.

"Hey, guys!" Emmett's cousin Romy walks up, dressed in

yoga pants and a T-shirt tied behind her back. Another family member joining us. I'm sensing a theme.

"Romy," I say, "are you joining the class too?"

"Sure am!" Her overexcitement tells me they were all worried I wouldn't have anyone in class, and that's why she's here. I'm positive Gillian is behind this.

One after another, Emmett's cousins walk toward the studio.

Even Sadie, who is holding her stomach. "I heard yoga was good for the baby."

Emmett coughs, and I shoot him my best scathing look to shut the fuck up before he outs me.

We huddle in a circle as a few guests trickle in, smiling and saying hello. I've never had people show up like this for me. Sure, Gillian and Koa, when he's not off finding himself, but the Noughton brothers and the cousins are all so tight, it's kind of scary.

"I'm so excited. Another girl at the house," Romy says with a big smile.

"Thanks for having me. I swear I won't be a house guest for long," I assure her, Poppy, and Scarlett. Lottie is the only female cousin not here because she runs The Harvest Depot, and it's open right now.

"It's going to be so much fun. And I promise our couch is so comfortable. I've fallen asleep there many a night and just decided to stay there," Poppy adds.

"The couch?" Emmett asks with clear judgment.

"Shouldn't you be working?" Gillian asks in a tone that makes it clear she disapproves.

"I'm on break. You can't sleep on their couch," he says to me.

"Why can't she?" Romy asks. "Last I checked, you weren't looking for a roommate."

All the women laugh except for Gillian and me. She's

staring at Emmett as if she wants to slice his throat. I've never seen Gillian so protective. Does she know something about him I don't? Everyone probably knows Emmett Noughton is the biggest playboy in Willowbrook. That's exactly why I'd never go for him. I promised myself when I left Chicago that I was done with my usual type, which is basically Emmett.

"I understand that Bruce said she should live with you, but I was able to make her more suitable arrangements," my sister says.

"Suitable? A couch?" Emmett raises his dark eyebrows. He's so expressive with his facial features, and I like that because it's easy to tell what he's thinking.

"Living with other women, not a bachelor." Gillian crosses her arms.

"I should get ready for the class." I thumb at the studio door.

"In my house, she'd have her own room. Her own space." Emmett's stance moves wider, and that easygoing persona he usually has is fraying at the edges the longer this continues.

"I'm gonna go set up my mat," Scarlett says. She, Romy, and Poppy walk into the studio.

I lean in close. "Will the two of you just stop?" I whisper. "It's my decision and a couch is fine." I glare at Emmett.

"It isn't fine," he says, and I double down on my death stare. He shakes his head. "I'll never understand women."

"Emmett, I love you, but go back to work." Gillian pats his shoulder. "Come on, let's go." She swings her arm around my shoulders, and I give Emmett one fleeting look, hoping to convey to him to keep quiet, before allowing Gillian to lead me into the studio.

With the addition of all the cousins who Gillian probably bribed to come here, it's actually full. I go to the front of the room, and it's nice to be back in my element. Leaving my established studio in Chicago was one of the hardest things I've ever done, but Chad gave me no choice.

Turning on the music, I begin my class, feeling a calm that rarely comes over me except when I'm teaching.

After my class was finished, Scarlett went on and on about how she was going to recruit more people from neighboring towns, and eventually, we could incorporate a lot more things with health and wellness on the ranch. It was as if she was scared I'll leave. Little does she know I have nowhere to go.

I walk out of The Getaway Lodge and stare at the sky, allowing the sun to heat my skin. It's still spring though, so I zip up my sweatshirt.

"You're not going to sleep on a couch."

I turn to my right and find Emmett pushing himself off the wall.

"Do you ever work?" I ask, walking again to get away from any prying ears. I don't trust Emmett to keep my secret quiet.

"It's a benefit of being one of the owners." He follows me toward the walking path through the grounds.

"And Jude? His days are just as leisurely?"

"Well, he takes a long lunch if you know what I mean." He knocks his shoulder against mine.

I say nothing, but Emmett is loud. Like, the loudest person I've ever met. So distance from everyone is my friend right now. Once we're hidden by some of the trees, and I don't see anyone, I stop.

He draws back, surprised by my sudden stop.

"Listen, whatever you think you know, you don't."

His eyes fall to my stomach.

"Stop doing that."

"I'm not doing anything."

I lean in close. "It was just nerves. I'm not... you know."

He laughs and shakes his head. "I get that a lot of people around here underestimate me, but I know I'm right. You're preg—"

I cover his mouth with my hand. "Shut up." I look around us. He nips at my fingers, and I pull back, shaking my hand at my side. "What the hell?" I scour the area one more time. "Listen. You can't tell anyone, okay?"

"So, I was right?" He beams. "Total honesty, I figured—you can't lie very well—but for a second, I thought maybe I wasn't piecing the puzzle together correctly, you know?"

"Emmett..." I attempt to maintain some patience with him by drawing in a deep breath. "Please, I'm asking you not to say anything."

He crosses his arms, bringing one hand up to his mouth and tapping his pointer finger on his bottom lip. His biceps bulge, and his lips look kissable, and his eyes, the way they're watching me... this man is my kryptonite. He always has been. "On one condition."

I huff. "What do you want? I can't cook. I suck at cleaning. I don't have anything to offer you, I promise."

He stares at the sky. "Beautiful day, right?"

"Emmett," I say with a growl, losing my patience.

His million-dollar smile lands on me, and it feels... unsettling. "Move in with me."

I throw my hands up at my sides and walk again. Why the hell would he want that? How would it benefit him? Then the reason flickers through my pregnancy brain, and I circle back to him. "I am not going to sleep with you whenever you want just so you don't tell anyone I'm pregnant."

I've never seen Emmett short of a response, but his mouth slowly falls open, and there's hurt in his eyes. "Is that what you think of me?"

Oh, for hell's sake. I cannot handle this right now. "Just... why then?"

"Because I'm not the type of guy to let a pregnant woman sleep on a couch, share a bathroom, and have no privacy of her own."

"So, no sex then?"

He shakes his head. "I don't need to swindle deals to make a beautiful woman sleep with me."

I hate the way the word beautiful repeats in my head. "For real, though, how does this benefit you?"

He shrugs. "Told you. Peace of mind."

My tense exterior slips, and I sigh, allowing the weight of all my problems to crumble around me for just a moment because who is this version of Emmett Noughton? Maybe he's not the guy I thought he was. Either that or there's some angle I can't figure out. "But why do you need peace of mind where I'm concerned?"

"I'm not sure I have an answer. Or at least not a logical one. You clearly don't like me, and allowing you to live in my house might feel like a torture chamber for me, thanks to your hormones. I get that I can be annoying, but it's obvious you don't want to tell Gillian or anyone else. I understand feeling judged or whatever. And I just... I don't know, just say yes, though."

Something in me softens a bit. "I should do something for you. For letting me live there."

He shakes his head. "Not necessary."

"Can we really do this?" I'm unsure if I can coexist with him, but what he's offering with no strings attached sounds nice. I want a spot of my own to reflect on the choices I've made and what my future will look like. The couch at the girls' house is a great offer, but Emmett's does sound nicer.

"I guess we'll see. You'll probably be in the bathroom throwing up most of the time."

I roll my eyes.

"You really have to start getting my humor. Otherwise, we're going to be in a lot of fights, roomie."

I walk back in the direction of my car. "Emmett?"

"Yeah," he says in a quiet voice like mine.

"Thanks."

"Ah." He puts his arm around my shoulders and tugs me into his side. "Just call me Prince Charming."

What did I sign myself up for?

Chapter Eleven

EMMETT

Briar pulls up in her car in front of my house, and Gillian is in the front seat. Ben also drove over—probably to run interference. I'm not sure.

"I don't get it. You make a bet with me, and you move her in here after Gillian arranged a spot for her at the girls' house?" Ben crosses his arms, watching Briar park her car next to my truck.

"I think it's extreme that Gilly Bean wanted her to sleep on a couch when I have three empty bedrooms here."

"She's worried that only one bedroom will be used," Ben says, stepping off my porch to grab Briar's stuff.

I jog down, too. "What's the big issue if I did hook up with her? Your fiancée is going to extreme measures."

"She's protective."

"Protective? She acts like Briar is an innocent cub she's releasing into the wild."

Ben stops and places his hand on my chest. Here we go. "Just remember the bet, okay? Hands off, and you'll get your little dude ranch."

I stare down at his hand, ready to remind him that he

might be a retired professional football player, but I'm bigger and stronger than him now.

He pulls back his hand. "Please," he says, without sounding genuine in the slightest.

"I told you once, and I'll tell you again, you don't have anything to worry about." Especially now that I know she's pregnant with another man's child.

"Just make sure of it. Gillian's happiness is the most important to me. You fuck with that, and you fuck with me."

I hold up my hands and shake them. "Ohhh...you're scaring me."

"Fuck," he mumbles, but he smacks on an exaggerated smile when he turns back toward the car. "Hey, you two."

Briar climbs out. The trunk pops open, and Briar moves to get a box.

"How nice of you to help, Ben," Gillian says. "I know you have track practice."

"This is more important." He bends down and kisses her.

"And you're welcome, Gilly Bean." I put my hand on Briar's arm. "Let the men get it. You just sit there and look pretty."

"Oh no, you didn't," Gillian says.

"Really, I'm fine." Briar's teeth are clenched, and she's giving me that look that says she wants to cut off my dick.

"Ben and I are here to help. There are drinks in the kitchen."

"Fine, come on, Briar. Rarely is Emmett such a gentleman, so let's take advantage," Gillian says.

I'm impressed that I got Gillian to go along with it by acting like a chauvinist. I thought she'd tell Ben and me to have a seat, and she'd carry two boxes at once.

One look at the boxes that are barely taped, and I wonder how fast Briar moved out of her place in Chicago.

"Is this a produce box?" Ben asks.

"Yeah, and it looks like she just threw stuff in there." There's a picture frame, cords, pens, notepads. "Why did she move back again?"

Ben shrugs, putting the produce box on top of another box that looks as if it's about to disintegrate. "Gillian hasn't told me, and I'm wondering if maybe she doesn't know because when I ask for specifics, she says Briar just told her she had to get out of Chicago."

We walk up the porch steps and inside.

"Who ordered grapes?" I ask the girls because of the box.

No one laughs. Gillian used to find me funny, but I guess not now that her sister is moving into my house.

"Did you pick a bedroom?" I ask Briar.

Ben repositions his boxes, wincing and sighing. Briar clearly hasn't picked a room, from the blank look on her face.

"Go on up and pick one."

She looks at Gillian, and they both get up.

"You've turned over a leaf. Now you're treating her like a princess." Gillian walks by the two of us and heads upstairs with Briar right after her.

I can't wait to see what kind of person Briar is without Gillian around.

Thankfully, Ben blocks me from seeing Briar's ass by walking up the stairs before me.

When we reach the top, the two women are discussing closet space.

"You should take this one," Gillian says. No coincidence, I'm sure, that it's the farthest from my bedroom.

"Yeah, but this one has the en suite, and it has the walk-in closet." Briar gravitates toward the bedroom right next to mine.

"I'm sure you don't want to share a wall with him," Gillian says.

"Can we hurry this up?" Ben repositions the boxes again, almost dropping them.

"When did I become just 'him?'" I ask.

Gillian glances over but doesn't really look at me, and she doesn't answer my question.

"This one, Ben, thanks." Briar points at the one where our beds will share a wall.

I bite the inside of my cheek and look away because trying not to look at Gillian is like driving by a car on the side of the road pulled over by the police after they flashed their lights and sped by you. It's oddly satisfying.

"Are you sure?" Gillian asks.

"She's sure," Ben says and walks by his soon-to-be wife, placing the boxes on the floor.

I furnished all the rooms one by one over the years I've lived here. Not that I get a ton of visitors, but I like it feeling like a home instead of vacant rooms. So she's got a queen bed, a dresser, and a vanity in the room she chose.

"I love the paint color," Briar says.

"It's Meet Cute."

"I'm sorry?" she asks.

"The paint color. It's called Meet Cute." I point at the blush color on the wall.

Gillian grunts and stares at Ben.

"I'm gonna go get more boxes," he says, fleeing the room like a fly escaping from a fly swatter.

"Let's start unpacking," Gillian says and eyes me. Man, I am not her favorite person these days.

"No, Gill, I'll get there. I barely have anything," Briar says.

While they hash it out, I jog down the stairs to get more boxes. The sooner we get Briar moved in, the quicker Gillian will leave.

I walk out of the house and back to the car. Ben is tripling the boxes up as if he's a professional mover.

"You're going to kill your back."

"Cut the shit," Ben says, not moving.

Are we playing a game of who can hold the most weight?

I grab four boxes, but they're smaller. One has a diaper logo on the side, and I think about how ironic that is. "What shit? About your back?"

"No, the whole meet-cute thing. Gillian is going to be spying on you with binoculars if you don't tone it down on the come-ons."

"Come-ons? It's really the paint color. Want to see the can?"

"And you remember this, why?"

I walk by Ben because I've had enough of this bullshit with Ben and Gillian. "Trust me, I'm not trying to come on to her."

For reasons I won't say. Do I wish Briar wasn't hot as hell? It would make my life a lot easier, but Briar being pregnant puts her in a category I'm not ready for.

He doesn't say anything else, and when we get to the top of the stairs, the two women are hugging.

"What's going on?" Ben asks, but walks to the bedroom.

Ben and I share a look but don't say anything. I follow him into the bedroom because I'm not good with girl shit. I grew up with two brothers, and sure, I had my cousins, but they never lived with me.

For whatever reason, the girls don't answer Ben's question, so we move on.

"There's only one box left," Ben says. "In the back seat."

Briar circles out of Gillian's arms. "I can get that one."

Ben steps back, running into me because Briar pushes him back with her hand on his chest.

Is the pregnancy test in there? What's the secret in that box? I hate the fact I'm curious as fuck. I've never been able to control myself.

"I'll get it," I say, walking around Ben, thinking she'll trust me since I already know her secret, but she steps in front of me, and her delicate hand presses to my chest.

I don't draw back because I kind of like it. If only Briar could rake her nails down my abs and dip those fingers under the waistband of my jeans.

Bad dick, stop overriding my brain.

"I said I'll get it." She moves to the stairs.

Gillian gives us a look as though one of us better get our ass down there and get that box.

Ben goes, and I'm about to follow when Gillian's hand lands on my chest. What the hell? At least I don't get the same reaction to her as I did with Briar.

"Listen, I know I'm being hard on you and taking things out on you."

I raise my eyebrows because yes, she is.

"I'm sorry, I'm protective of Briar. She didn't have an easy childhood." She nods toward the stairs where her sister just went. "Her mom didn't die, she left her. Me and you, we understand what it feels like when your mother dies, but her mom decided to take herself out of the picture. To not see Briar grow up and accomplish all that she has. And my dad was great, but he worked all the time to support us. I see she's hurting, but she hasn't opened up to me yet. I know there was a guy, but that's all I know. And sure, you'd be a great rebound—"

"Ah, thanks, Gilly Bean," I say, bringing comedy in because I don't want to know this shit.

"But she needs stability, calm, and a place to pick herself up. I don't want lust mixed into that equation. I apologize for being so hard on you."

"Why?"

"Why what?" she asks.

"Why didn't you just say this from the start? Instead of treating me like crap?"

She checks the stairs again. "I acted on instinct, like a new mom with a baby. It's hard, but I don't imagine you'll understand."

"I'm your brother-in-law. I've always had your back, and I'll continue to. Trust me on this. I won't hurt her," I say, hoping that puts her at peace.

She blows out a breath. "Okay. Call me if it gets out of your hands."

"If she gets out of my hands?" I laugh. She doesn't. "No one gets my humor anymore."

"Gill, I gotta go," Ben calls from downstairs. "Emmett, come get the box. She's acting like an armored truck driver protecting a million dollars."

We walk down the stairs, and I head outside.

"I can stay and unpack," Gillian says to Briar.

"I've got it. I'm going to unpack and probably go grocery shopping."

"I can go with," Gillian says.

Briar blows out a breath but smiles. "I'm a big girl." She hugs her sister.

"Not a good look when the coach is late," Ben says.

Gillian stands there, staring at both of us. I wink to tell her I have it handled, but she still looks like a creepy stalker.

"Go, Gill. I'll call you." Briar waves.

"Okay, yeah." Gillian walks backward toward Ben's truck.

"She'll be about one hundred footsteps away." I'm trying to give Gillian peace of mind, but she nibbles her bottom lip.

Ben gets out of the truck, picks Gillian up from behind, and takes her to the truck. Briar and I laugh.

"What are you doing?" Gillian says.

"Practicing for when we drop Clayton off at college," Ben

says, putting her in the passenger seat of the truck. "See you, guys." He waves.

We watch him pull away, Gillian acting as if she just left her sister in Antarctica, waving with a terrified expression.

"Just you and me," I say.

Briar reaches into the back seat of her car, but I place my hands on her hips to slide her over. Jesus, it's as though her hips were made for my hands. I quickly remove my hands, shaking them out at my sides. Grabbing the box, I haul my ass to the house to get myself under control. It's just lust, and I'm an adult and can control myself.

"Aunt Briar!" Clayton walks through the row of trees that separates my house from Ben's.

I stop for a second to see her walk toward him before I go into the house and up to her bedroom. I'm about to drop the box on the floor when the bottom falls out of it. Spiral notebooks, yearbooks, and I think keepsakes tumble to the floor.

I squat down and fix the bottom of the box, then pile everything back in the box. Then I see scribbling in girl's handwriting that says, *Mrs. Emmett Noughton.*

What the fuck?

I thumb through the notebook, and there's so much more. *I love Emmett. Briar and Emmett 4 ever.* The doodles and scribbles are all over the notebooks, with hearts around my name.

Briar Adams had a crush on me in high school. Which makes me wonder—how did she go from liking me to hating me?

Chapter Twelve

BRIAR

Clayton walks over, his phone in his hands. "Mom said you might need some help."

I shake my head. Does Gillian realize that at some point, I will be left alone with Emmett?

"No, I don't. Emmett just took up the last box." A box that holds all my high school keepsakes. A box I really would've preferred to carry myself. The thought of Emmett seeing all the notebooks and yearbooks with hearts over his picture... I'd rather die. "You can go home and do whatever you were doing."

"Thanks. My girlfriend..."

"Yeah, go, no problem. Thanks, though."

"Sure thing."

Clayton walks back on the trail he came from. As long as I'm staying here, Gillian will wear that trail down to dust.

I walk up the porch steps, slide into the house, and head up the stairs. Emmett's coming back down.

"All set," he says, thumbing toward my bedroom.

"Oh great. Thanks." I scour his facial expression, hoping he didn't snoop in the box, looking for some sign that he saw the secret I'm taking to my grave. Because there's more to that crush that I am not about to confess to anyone. Especially my new roommate.

Instead of continuing up the stairs, I head back down so we can discuss our living arrangement.

Emmett's house is a lot nicer than I expected. I assumed he lived like a bachelor with dirty dishes in the sink, trash on the countertops and floor. I figured as payback for me living here, I'd clean his house. With the exception of his bathroom, of course. But by the look of things, there's no need for me to be his housekeeper. The only thing that shows he's a bachelor is that his walls are completely bare. There's not one picture, or anything hung up.

Emmett goes to the fridge and grabs a water, standing by the counter. His kitchen isn't as modern as Ben and Gillian's, but it's got a charm theirs doesn't.

"Do you have a house cleaner?" I ask, awkwardly standing in the large opening from his kitchen to his family room. Whereas Ben and Gillian's home is open concept, there's a clear distinction between the rooms in Emmett's house.

"Do you think I can't clean?" The bottle indents as he swallows more water.

"Awfully thirsty for carrying a few boxes up the stairs."

He looks down at me with the bottle still on his lips, but there's humor in his eyes.

"Nice," he says once he finishes the entire bottle and crushes it with his hands. "Rule number one, crush the bottles, that way more can fit in the recycling can."

"That's the number one rule you want to go with?" I step into the kitchen fully, leaning against his small butcher block island.

"Recycling is important to me," he says. "Your turn to make a rule now."

"You're letting me stay here. I don't get to make rules."

He opens the fridge and pulls out another water. He's really ingesting a lot of water but watching his Adam's apple bounce as he swallows is strangely erotic. Not that I would admit that to anyone. His forearms bulge as he twists off the cap.

Get a grip, Briar. He's your new roommate, and you're pregnant with another man's baby. This is platonic. That's all it'll ever be.

He holds the water bottle out to me. "Here, you should hydrate."

I chuckle, and he joins in with his own laughter. "Is that your prenatal advice?"

"I don't know, but it seems like everything you drink and eat goes to the baby, so you have to drink twice the amount of water."

I accept the water and take a sip, which helps calm down my libido. "Thanks."

"So?" He arches a dark eyebrow.

"So what?"

"What's your rule?"

"Um... it seems odd making a rule when it's your house."

"I'm an equal opportunity guy, so go ahead before I take it back." He pulls a pack of ground beef from the fridge. "Are you a vegetarian?"

"Because I'm a yoga instructor?"

His head rocks back, and he shakes it. "No. It was just a question. Man, take a few bricks down off that fortress you've built around yourself."

I hate that I'm warming to him. Maybe it's because he's kept my secret so far, plus he offered me a place to stay with a bedroom and bathroom all of my own. "What are you making?"

"I'm trying to replicate my dad's burgers."

"Why?" I round the island and take the stool on the far end, watching him take out a bowl and some seasonings.

He shrugs. "I just like figuring shit out." He eyes me for a second, dumping the ground beef into the bowl. "I'm not a big secret guy."

"Oh—"

He puts up his hand. "I didn't mean it like that. I just want to figure this out because it's a childhood memory. My dad makes these burgers every time we celebrate or as a reward or for bribery." His mouth twists and his eyebrows raise. "Lately, it's been about bribery."

"I can help."

He shakes his head. "First you need to give me a rule."

I place my chin in my hand. "How do I top crushing the bottles down for recycling?"

He points at me. "I like this version of you."

"Which version?"

"Relaxed... nice." His head tilts. "Are you going to tell me why you hate me?"

That wall I keep around myself reinforces with another layer of cement. "Nope."

He nods. "But you're starting to like me."

He's right, but I'm not telling him that. How could the hatred I've let fester over the years not diminish with this adult version of him? His confidence is what attracted me to him in high school. The way he walked the halls and was friendly with everyone. He was four years older, and I wasn't alone with my crush. Most girls at school liked Emmett.

"Not sure why you think that."

"I love the act. Deny until proven wrong." He grabs some seasoning, measures, and writes it down in a notebook. So meticulous and calculating. Two traits I didn't know Emmett possessed.

"You've surprised me," I admit, regretting my words immediately.

He looks at me from the corner of his eye, and the cutest smile slowly creases his lips. "Good." Then he winks, which I realize creates a tornado of butterflies in my stomach.

We sit in silence while I watch him continue to try to master the recipe. I'm so mesmerized that I don't realize he asked a question until his hands stop moving. My gaze flows up his arms, past his broad shoulders, to his eyes pinned on me.

"I'm sorry?"

"Rule. Time for you to come up with one."

"Well, I could say the toilet seat, but I'll probably only use my bathroom upstairs. You keep a clean house. I do have a question though."

"Shoot." He forms the meat into balls.

"Obviously, you'll bring women home—"

"Why do you think that?" He smirks and goes to the sink, washing his hands.

"Oh please."

"I'll let you in on a little secret, what with me knowing your big one." He grabs the paper towels and leans against his counter, crossing his ankles, his gaze on me.

"You don't—"

"I don't bring women home. Anymore."

He has to be lying. This is a game he's playing. Seeing if I'll bite. "Yeah right."

He tosses the paper towel into the trash as if he's shooting a basketball, then takes the tray to the stove. He's got it down perfectly, taking out a flat frying pan with small edges to catch the grease. "I'm serious. Not saying I've never done it, but I'm not big on bringing women to the ranch. And you'll think I'm ass when I tell you this, but they get clingy and think it means more than it does. I don't want to give them the wrong idea. I never string women along, but something about bringing them home seems to make them think it means more than it does, even when I tell them otherwise beforehand."

It's clear he's serious, so I nod.

"So, how about rule number two is a mutual one. No women for me and no men for you."

I raise my eyebrows, looking down at my stomach. "I'm done in the guy department, maybe forever. But I can bring a woman home?"

He glances over his shoulder at me. "Only if rule number three is that I get to watch."

I giggle, and it feels really good to laugh and not be so caught up in Chad and all the bullshit that went down. "Deal, but I wouldn't get your hopes up."

"If it changes, let me know." He smashes the burgers down with the spatula and the fat sizzles.

I'm not sure if they'll taste like his dad's, since I've never had them, but my mouth waters and my stomach growls. I watch him move around the kitchen, grabbing buns, buttering them, and putting them on another frying pan on the stove.

While waiting, he pulls out condiments. "Help yourself to whatever I have. Although I do have Jensen cook for me a lot."

"Oh no, I'll go grocery shopping."

"Jensen will cook for you too."

"If Darla makes him."

He laughs. "She likes you a lot, you know that, right?"

"Darla? Well, she seems to like everyone." I sip my water, then spin the bottle around.

"Wren told Bennett she wants to be like you when she grows up."

I cough out a laugh. "Wait until she finds out what I've done with my life."

"She likes you because you don't treat her like she's a little kid." He stops cooking, plates the burgers, and turns off the burners. "I know you don't want to talk about it, and if you never do, that's fine. But if you do, I'm happy to listen."

"I'm not good with children. I have no idea how I'll raise this one." I run my hand over my flat stomach.

He gives me a sad smile. I'm sure he believes the same thing. I'm treading water with a hurricane on its way to me, and there's no one to throw me a life vest.

"Come on, we're eating on the deck."

He grabs the plates and walks out a door off his kitchen where there is a porch overlooking the lake. I missed it coming from the other side of the house. He's got a small table and some comfortable patio furniture.

"This is nice," I say.

"It's my favorite place, so feel special that I'm sharing it with you." He places everything on the table. On his way back into the house, he squeezes my shoulder. "It will all work out. I promise."

Tears sting my eyes as he disappears inside. I suck them back because no matter what happens, I'll handle it. I always do. But damn it, Emmett Noughton has evolved into a mature man he seems to hide from everyone. The question is why? And also, why is he being so nice to me?

Chapter Thirteen

EMMETT

Sometimes, I wish my curiosity would take a fucking vacation.

I'm in the crawl space of my basement, grabbing the box my dad gave me when I moved out. It holds all my high school shit. My yearbooks, varsity letters, awards, accolades, etc. I don't remember Briar very well from high school, other than that she was Gillian's younger sister, and by then, Gillian and Ben had broken up, and he was away at college.

Pulling my senior yearbook out, I flip through the freshman class, searching for her. She's on the first page, and this is the Briar I remember. She's wearing braces, her hair is super short and not very styled, and her glasses are way too big on her face. But it's how young she looks that takes me back. Then again, she was four years younger than me.

Still, no memories surface, and I have to wonder why I'd be an asshole to a young girl. Especially Gillian's sister. Because that's the only reason I can think of that would make her hate me. I shake my head and shut the yearbook, then put everything back before climbing the stairs to return to the main level.

My phone vibrates in my pocket, and I pull it out to find a text from Lottie.

Can you do me a favor?

This is one part of being the "immature one" that I hate. Lottie needs something delivered to The Harvest Depot, and since Bennett has Wren, and Jensen spends all his damn time in the kitchen, she messages me.

What?

Can you do a pickup at Laurel's? She was supposed to deliver them to me, but she's slammed.

I'm always the fucking gopher. Like I have no damn life except to do the shit no one else wants to do.

Sure.

I jog up the stairs from the basement and swipe my keys off the table.

Briar is sitting on the couch with her laptop and her legs stretched out. Her blonde hair is in a messy bun on top of her head. She really is sexy as hell, and I can't believe she's fucking pregnant with what I'm assuming is some douchebag's baby since she's here and not in Chicago with him. I have a ton of questions, but I'm not about to ask them. It's none of my business.

She glances at me with red-rimmed eyes, and my stomach clenches. I loved hearing her giggle the other day, but after that, I haven't seen a lot of emotion from her. I get that she's dealing with a lot of shit I can't imagine. I was young when

Gillian had Clayton, but I remember that she seemed the same —no smiles until Clayton was born.

"Busy?" I ask.

"Just looking some stuff up." Her finger scrolls over the touchpad of the laptop.

"Want to go for a ride?" I figure it will be good to get her away from here and out of her head.

She quirks an eyebrow. "Am I a dog?"

A laugh escapes because her one-liners kill me, especially when she doesn't show any emotion.

"I'll roll the window down for you and everything."

She shuts her laptop and gets up. "Can we hit a drive-through for a doggie treat?"

She slides on her sweatshirt, and I try not to concentrate on how her tits are snug in a sports bra. She's torturing me daily with her tight clothes.

"Maybe I'll take you to the doggie park too."

"Today is the best day ever." She puts her purse over her arm and walks toward the screen door. "No leash?"

"That's for the bedroom later," I say, and her face explodes into the best smile.

Why does that do something to my heart? Why do I want to make this better for her? I barely know her.

We walk out to my truck, and I open the door for her. She looks surprised, but I choose to ignore the fact that she doesn't have high expectations of me. After I climb into the driver's seat, she buckles herself in.

"I forgot how everyone drives trucks here," she says, wiggling in the cushy seat. The thing I love about pickups is the room inside the cab.

"What do they drive in Chicago?" I back out of my drive with my hand on the back of her headrest while I look over my shoulder, then I head toward the small road to leave the ranch.

"A lot of sports cars and SUVs. Minivans, but that's mostly families."

"Which do you prefer—Chicago or Willowbrook?" I dare ask, inching closer to the subject of why she left.

"I'm not sure. I loved Chicago when I first got there. The tall buildings and the millions of people who don't know or care who you are as you walk by. And the food. God, the food was so good." Her eyes flutter closed as if she's remembering something, and for a second, I wonder what she looks like when she comes.

Stop. It. Now.

"What was your favorite?"

"Pasta. I usually try not to eat too much of it, but there was this place on the corner by my apartment building. Fresh homemade noodles, and they had this butter garlic cream sauce I'd try not to eat because once I did, I'd crave it for a week straight." She laughs, and her head lolls my way. "If you ever go to Chicago, go to Bella Bites."

"Will do."

"And they had these garlic bread sticks. Ever since I got pregnant, it's all I want. Pasta. Any kind. He or she isn't picky." She runs her hand over her stomach.

I've seen her do that a few times in the week she's lived with me. Almost as if she's growing used to the idea of being a mother.

"Well, I can't offer you much here. But I'll take you to By The Slice, and we can get a cheeseburger pizza. They have garlic bread and some marinara pasta that's probably just sauce from a jar."

"I haven't had a cheeseburger pizza since I moved away from here. The pizza from Chicago is deep dish with a lot of cheese and sauce. It's good, but I'll take the cheeseburger pizza over that any day."

I raise my fist. "Nebraska for the win."

I drive us to Willowbrook's small downtown and park along the small square in front of Laurel's bakery. Sure enough, she's got a line out the door.

"I feel bad. Gillian said I could take her hours here, and I never answered her about it. Maybe I should stay and help." She grabs the handle and exits the vehicle.

I meet her in front of my truck. "Is it safe to be around all those ovens and mixers?"

Her forehead wrinkles. "I'm not five, Emmett."

"I'm just saying, what if your stomach bumps into a hot sheet or something?"

She shakes her head, laughing at me. "You're being protective of me?"

"Yeah, you wish," I say like a teenage boy trying to be mean to the girl he likes.

The truth is, women are foreign beings to me. My mom died when I was two years old, and I have no memories of her. Dad never remarried. I figured out young how to turn a woman on. Kimmy, the preacher's daughter, gave me some lessons I still use today. But emotionally, fuck, I don't even know how to be a friend to a woman.

We slip by the large line of people. Laurel and Gillian are going in opposite directions behind the counter, trying to fill orders.

"Are cupcakes going extinct?" I ask as we approach the side of the counter.

Neither Laurel nor Gillian laugh, but Briar does. I kind of like that.

"Laurel made Oatmeal Creme Pie Cupcakes, and I think she put heroin in them or something because she can't keep up with the demand."

"Oh, they're so good, Emmett," Mr. Torres, who's at the front of the line, says. "Who are you?" he asks, looking at Briar.

Gillian uses her sonic hearing and answers his question. "That's my sister, Briar."

"Oh, little Briar. Do you remember story time?"

Briar smiles sweetly. Not one I've ever seen her use. It's her fake smile. "I do. The way you'd act out all the characters, even the women."

"Someone had to be the princess and queen."

Laurel calls, "Next."

"Oh, it's my turn." Mr. Torres looks like he did when he acted out the characters at story time.

"I'm here to pick up for Lottie," I say.

"You get what you need and go. I'll stay to help," Briar says. "I'm sure Gillian can drive me home."

I thought we were going to have lunch. I try to push away the disappointment I feel.

"Neither one you have to stay. We're about to sell out." She places them in the display case. "Last dozen."

Groans ring out in the storefront. One person tells the person behind them, and quickly, the line outside disperses, people looking pissed off as they leave.

"Good, we're going to lunch then," I say.

Gillian stops checking out Mr. Torres and glares at me.

"I can't fuck her on the table in the middle of the restaurant. It's lunch."

Gillian looks away from me, finishing the sale with Mr. Torres.

"Don't talk like that in my store," Laurel reprimands me.

Mrs. VanKamp just gave me that look I got when I was in trouble in kindergarten. Not much has changed.

"Sorry. Don't worry, I'll drop off the goods to Lottie before we grab something to eat."

"Now that we're sold out, Gillian can drop them off." Laurel puts her hand on Gillian's shoulder.

"I just made your favorite, Briar. Chicken pot pies. No

need to go out to lunch—come over to our house," Gillian says.

Laurel blows out a breath and runs her hand down Briar's arm as if she's consoling her.

"Sorry, Gill, but Emmett brought up cheeseburger pizza, and I haven't had it since I returned. I think I'd like to go there," Briar says.

Gillian hands the change to Mr. Torres and turns to us, her hip resting on the counter and her arms crossed.

"Let them go, Gill," Laurel says. "I'll come over for some pot pies."

"Go on then," Gillian says, clearly not pleased.

You don't have to tell me twice. I'm on my way to the door before I realize Briar isn't with me. She's hugging Gillian and whispering something to her. She finally joins me, and we make our way inside the truck.

"Why is she so worried about something happening between us?" I start the truck.

I talked with Gillian and understood her worry, but it's a little extreme that she thinks I have zero control over my dick.

Briar shrugs. "You have a reputation. She knows about Chad. Not everything, but that he hurt me."

My hands tighten on the steering wheel. So, the douchebag has a name.

"Hurt you?" I try to keep my voice even-keeled, but if he hit her, I'll be showing up at every damn door in Chicago that has someone named Chad living there until I find him.

"Heartbreak. I loved him, or so I thought. Can we just go?"

I pull out of the parking spot and head toward By The Slice. "So, what do you think my reputation is?" At the stoplight, I glance over to see her shrug.

"I haven't lived here in a long time, but when I did, you were always with a girl, and I don't mean dating."

"Yeah..." I don't finish my sentence. The part of me who hooks up is a complicated part that even I don't fully understand. Mostly because I don't like to psychoanalyze myself and how fucked up it is that I can't have a normal relationship like my brothers.

"Care to elaborate?" she asks.

"As soon as you do." I side-eye her, and she turns toward the window.

"I'm starving. How much longer?"

I laugh because we're both messed up, and neither one of us wants to address our issues. And that works perfectly for me.

Chapter Fourteen

BRIAR

After my afternoon class, I head back to Emmett's, ready to take a shower. Maybe I'll make him dinner as a thank you for being way nicer than I expected. My expectations of what it would be like living with Emmett compared to what it's actually like are as opposite as you can get.

He didn't lie about cooking. Most of our meals come from Jensen, but I'm not complaining. Emmett leaves early to work the farm, but he's never missed a breakfast with Wren. At night, he watches television, or he's on his computer, writing things down. Last Saturday, he went out, but he was home by midnight, since I heard his headboard hit the wall. He keeps his space, and I keep mine for the most part.

My phone rings in my bag, and I grab it. When will Gillian stop treating me like I'm thirteen?

"Gill? Thank God. Come and get me, Emmett showed me his pee pee." I use a fake distressed voice, trying to freak her out.

"Briar?"

I pull the phone back to make sure the voice I'm hearing is

actually who I think it is. Sure enough, the bastard is calling me.

"You need to lose this number." I click End but I don't dump the phone in my bag like I should.

It rings again, and I let it go to voicemail, but it rings again almost immediately.

I pick up. "Stop calling me. It's over."

"Wait!"

I don't say anything.

"Briar, I... I know I should've told you. But I never knew how."

"You had an entire year."

"I know." He's quiet, which he should be. Cheating bastard. "I didn't expect to fall for you, and when I did, I knew telling you would risk everything. I loved you... love you... you're my everything."

I hate that phrase. I'm not his everything. I was his regular hookup. His side piece. Only I didn't know it. All the trips, the dinners, the lazy Sunday mornings. It's too cliché now that I'm looking back at our relationship with a magnifying glass.

"Just stop. It's over. We're... over." I shift the phone to hang up.

"Where are you? Let me talk to you in person. I can't do this over the phone."

"You mean you can't manipulate me over the phone. Your charm isn't going to work, Chad." I sit on the porch steps of Emmett's house, thankful his truck isn't in the drive.

"I want to see you. I miss you."

"Miss my body, you mean?"

He always complimented me on how fit I was and how great the sex was because I'm so flexible. Now I know who I was being compared to.

"Yes... no... you know what I mean. I miss us."

I roll my eyes, bring my knees to my chest, and rest my forehead on them. "Well, I don't."

I'm lying, but not because I miss us. I miss who I thought we were and who I thought we were on our way to being.

"Yes, you do. How could you not? We were great together."

"That's your perception. Mine is different."

I hear a muffled sound. "One minute, Janice."

His secretary. "You're fucking the secretary now? How cliché can you get?"

"No, I have a call."

"Take the call, Chad. We have nothing else to say to one another."

"I'll fly to you tomorrow. Just tell me where you are."

The fact he doesn't even know where I'm from says how little we knew about one another. I hate hindsight, but when I look at our path to I love you, there's a trail of little red flags I was happy to ignore.

"Goddamn it, Janice, I said one minute."

"Bye, Chad. Lose this number." I hang up and clutch my phone.

The tickling in my nose starts. I don't want to cry. I've pushed the tears back so many times since I returned to Willowbrook, but hearing his voice stirs up all the guilt and betrayal.

Sure, our relationship wasn't ideal. He worked late, traveled a lot, but he always made up for that when he'd come to me right from the airport or after a late dinner, and he'd bring me cheesecake.

One tear falls, and the others immediately follow. My back racks with sobs as my hands try to catch every tear because Chad isn't worth them.

I hear a truck engine pull in, and I know it's Emmett. I

quickly sit up and run my fingers under my eyes. I hear him get out, and damn, I wish I was locked in my room. The last thing I want is for him to see me like this.

"Hey," he says, staring at me. "You okay?"

I nod unconvincingly. "I'm good."

He sits next to me, one step down, turning to rest his back on the railing of the stairs and look out at the lake. "So not sure if you're aware or not, but I'm not blind."

My shoulders sink, and my lips betray me in a small smile. "Can we ignore it?"

He nods. "Sure, if you want." He doesn't get up, continuing to stare at the lake.

"Why are you going so easy on me?" I shouldn't ask the question that's been plaguing me. He's never pushed me for any information.

At first, I don't think he's going to answer. He never even glances my way. "When your mom dies when you're two, everyone's always asking you how you're doing. Every milestone that she should've been there, you see the question in their eyes. 'Are you handling it okay?' Fuck. What the hell do they think? It's a stupid-ass question. One I shouldn't have just asked you." He chuckles. "I figure if you want to talk to me about it, you will. If you don't, that's okay."

"Thanks." I wrap my arms around my legs and follow his line of vision to the lake. It's so pretty here, I see why Ben returned and Jude and Emmett stayed. "He was married," I say, figuring he knows I'm pregnant, so he might as well know the whole story.

"That sucks." He doesn't turn to look at me.

"I didn't know. I swear I didn't."

"Didn't think you did." He brings one leg up and rests his forearm on it.

"I met him at a hotel. I was booked for a private lesson

with a client who was having her penthouse renovated. I was trying to get up to her room, but my client never put my name on the list, and she didn't answer her phone. He saw me arguing and came over to mediate. He was so charismatic, I was instantly attracted to him. He said he worked for the hotel and assured the receptionist he'd escort me to the room himself. Turns out he was some bigwig for the company who owned the hotel chain." I remember back to that day and how at the time, I'd thought my luck was changing. He was something good coming into my life. "His job was a great reason to always take me to hotels."

"Did you at least get unlimited room service?"

A sad sort of chuckle leaves my lips. "Do you take anything seriously?"

"Plenty."

"He flew me places, said how he lived out of a suitcase because of his job. I even believed the lame excuse that he liked my small apartment because it felt like home versus his bachelor pad. Do you know how bad it sucks to feel like a fool? To feel so stupid, you question your own intelligence?" I lean my head on the railing. "I was so naïve, so blind. And I've felt so guilty since I found out."

"Don't blame yourself."

"How can I not?" I swipe the tears falling down my face. "Oh my god, you don't need to hear any of this." I move to get up.

Despite the shame I felt when I found out that Chad was married, as soon as I found out I was pregnant, I knew I would have the baby. That no other choice was an option for me. I know firsthand what it feels like to be an unwanted child, and I couldn't give the baby up for adoption or have an abortion. Neither felt like the right decision for me.

And I knew after I'd decided to have the baby that I'd want

to do it here in Willowbrook. The cost of living is way less than in Chicago, and though I have friends there, I never really connected on a deeper level with them. I want to raise my child near my sister and in the town I grew up in.

"Sit down." Only when I do does he speak again. "My uncle Wade was sitting on our porch at my graduation party. The festivities had been dying down, and I was gonna go out with my friends to celebrate. I took the chair next to him, and to my surprise, he didn't ask me if I felt like something was missing that day because my mom wasn't there. He didn't ask me anything other than what I was going to do that night. Still today, I have no idea why at that moment, it felt right to tell someone what was going on in my head, but I sat with him for a half hour and told him all of the conflicting emotions I was dealing with. About my mom not being there. Waking up to random women in our house on Sunday mornings. The fear of staying on the farm forever. The fear of ever leaving the farm."

"Why did you decide to stay?" I ask—anything to get away from talking about me.

"Oh no, sweetheart, this is your confessional. And sorry that you've chosen me to spill your heart out to."

"Why are you sorry?"

"I'm not a counselor. I'm not going to hug you or tell you you'll find someone better. I'm not going to fill you up with hope because telling you those things, treating a relationship with an asshole as a loss, isn't what you need."

"What do I need?"

"That's for you to figure out. And you will. In time. Now, go on." His attention falls back to the lake, and I miss having his eyes on me.

"There isn't much to say beyond what I've already told you except that he doesn't know I'm pregnant."

Emmett nods.

"And I don't want him to know. I don't want him to be part of my life. He has his own kids that he left to spend time with me. What kind of father does that?"

"A shitty one."

"I want him as far away from me and our baby as possible." I run my hand over my stomach.

"Understandable."

"So, no advice? You're not an advice-giver either?" I ask.

He turns to me and smirks. "Anything I'm going to tell you, you already know for yourself. You know if you tell Gillian, she can help you the best out of anyone. She raised Clayton all by herself, and she found her way to believe in love and trust someone again. But you don't want to tell her, and you need to figure out why. Maybe you just need time."

My shoulders sag when I think of what it will be like telling my big sister everything. "I don't want to see her face. She'll be so disappointed in me."

"I think as long as I'm not the father, you're good on that front."

I chuckle and shake my head, some of the weight on my shoulders lifting. "Thanks."

"For what?"

"Making me laugh. Before I came here, I hadn't really laughed in a while. Until I moved in here with you."

"So, you don't hate me?" I register the surprise on his face.

"Nah, I still hate you," I say, lying through my teeth. As mad as I was, and even though I still harbor a lot of embarrassment about the past, he's shown me that he's not the person I thought he was. "You know, you haven't made one sexual comment to me since I moved in."

"Well, you're pregnant." He shrugs.

"So now I'm unattractive?"

He rises to his feet, picking up his cowboy hat. "Don't put words in my mouth."

He walks past me, and I want to grab his wrist and tug him down next to me, but I don't. The screen door bangs shut behind him, ending our conversation. I haven't wanted to follow Emmett so badly since I was a freshman in high school.

Who would've thought the man who annoys me the most would become my biggest confidant?

Chapter Fifteen

EMMETT

Jude and I are coming back from planting corn when Ben follows me into the barn.

"To what do I owe this visit?" I ask.

He runs his hand through his hair and looks at Jude. "How's the training going?"

"Fuck off. I've been planting corn for half my life." Nothing grates on me more than my brothers acting as though I'm an idiot.

"And he should be able to do it all by himself next year." Jude pats me on the shoulder.

"Or I'll be running the dude ranch," I say, staring at Ben. "How's that going anyway?"

Jude looks from me to Ben and back to me. "What am I missing?"

Ben blows out a breath and shoots Jude a look like he shouldn't ask.

"Ben and Gillian think I can't keep my dick in my pants." I cross my arms.

"And?" Jude asks, eyeing Ben.

"He wanted insurance so that I had an incentive not to touch Briar."

"And?" Jude's tone is one of exhaustion, which I do love bringing him to.

"Before we get to that, the horseshoe fitting video I did got more views than your gender reveal. I'm starting to get followers—"

"Jesus." Jude rocks his head back, stuffing his hands in his pockets and sending Ben a pleading look to save him.

"I told him I'd help him get the votes," Ben says.

"Votes?" Jude asks, eyes narrowing on Ben.

"For the dude farm," Ben says in the same exhausted voice as Jude.

"Fuck, you heard Dad." Jude's voice gets louder. "We have shit we need to get done around here. You need to learn my job."

"Which I would've known already if you'd taught me before you knocked up your best friend." I'm so sick of Jude acting as though it's my fault he hasn't let me take on more up to this point.

Jude charges me, but Ben gets in the middle, a hand on both of our chests.

"It's the truth," I say. "You've held back all the responsibilities as if I can't handle it."

"You can't!" Jude snaps.

I laugh—not a real one, a forced one that sounds almost sad because it's what I knew he thought the whole time. "Fuck off, Jude."

I walk out of the barn.

"Emmett," Jude calls.

I put my hand in the air, ready to leave them and disappear from this ranch, but anger overtakes me, and I spin around. "You don't even know me. You think so low of me? Fuck, I'm your brother."

"I just meant you don't take anything seriously. You—"

"Save it. I'm glad you both are so put together, so fucking perfect, and I'm the screw-up, right? The dumb one. The one who can't be responsible. Well, you guys don't know shit about me. The only thing you know about me is what I let you."

Neither of them says anything, and I spin back around.

"Emmett," Ben says, "that's not it. Just listen—"

"Yeah, I'm done listening." I walk toward my house, leaving my truck behind. I need to cool off before I get behind the wheel.

Taking my time on my walk, I take off my cowboy hat and hold it, purposely going out of my way to avoid walking by Jude and Sadie's. If she's home, she'll see I'm upset and try to fix it. There's no fixing that my brothers don't take me seriously or that anything I want doesn't matter as long as they're living their dreams.

I walk into my house, smelling garlic, and see Briar in my kitchen. She's wearing an apron that's too fucking cute, with her hair braided to the side of her head. There's music playing, and she's swinging her hips to the beat. The screen door shuts, giving me away, and she turns.

"Don't worry. When I get close to the stove, I put this on." She takes a blow-up inner tube off the counter and shimmies it over her head until it's around her waist.

Damn, I needed that laugh right now. It's as if she knew I just had a fight with my brothers.

"And I promise I'm not going to burn the garlic bread this time either."

I walk into the kitchen and wash my hands in the sink, looking at the garlic bread that's about to go in the oven. "Your famous garlic bread," I say, leaning along the counter, watching her as I dry my hands.

"Well, my mom's actually. It was about the only thing

either of us could cook." She opens the oven door and slides the tray into the oven.

I shrug. "It's something."

She smiles at me and nods. "Yeah, it is."

"What can I help with?" I toss the paper towel in the trash and wait for instructions.

"Nothing. This is my way of saying thanks for listening to me the other day. And also, for letting me stay here."

"I was brought up to help." I look at the stove and find a pot of boiling water.

She nudges me, pushing me away. "Go and sit. This is my meal to make."

"Hard bargain." I get a beer from the fridge, unscrew the top, and drop the cap in the trash before sitting on a stool.

"Enjoy that for me." She pours the pasta into the boiling water.

I take a long pull of my beer. "That one was for you."

She glances over her shoulder, and a feeling I've never felt washes over me. I'm watching a woman in my kitchen, preparing me dinner after I've had a grueling day on the ranch. It's not anything I've experienced before, and as crazy as it is, I don't hate it.

"So, what was your drink of choice?" I ask.

She stirs a wooden spoon through the water and rests it on top of the pot before walking over to the counter and leaning on it. "I love margaritas. Not frozen, on the rocks. Other than that, I'm a specials girl."

I sip my beer. "Specials girl?"

"The fruity drinks that are only available for the night, or for the week, or maybe the season. Those are my thing."

"Ahh... girly drinks."

She tilts her head and raises her eyebrows. "Specials."

I hold up my hands, not wanting to get into an argument with someone else today. I'm still stewing over the fight with

Jude and Ben. I'm not a confrontational person, which is probably how the whole situation blew up in the first place. I've let my feelings fester.

Briar pushes off the counter and goes to the stove, checking on the garlic bread. Contrary to most, I love surprises—the good kind obviously.

"How was your day at work? What do you do at the ranch? Chase and rope the cows?"

I chuckle. "Okay, tell me what you think happens on the ranch?"

She clues in on my sarcasm and pretend pouts. "You're making fun of me."

"Let's just say it was a shitty day, and I want to laugh."

She turns fully around, the wooden spoon in her hand, and stares at me for a moment. "I do need to pay you back for making me laugh."

"You don't want me calling the laugh police."

She stares at me blank-faced for a second.

"Okay, not my best line."

"No." She giggles. "All right. Well, I picture you on a horse every day, and you and Jude galloping around doing... I don't know."

I laugh.

"Maybe you're trying to keep the herd together, or you're in one of the rings, lassoing them by the head. Which looks painful by the way."

"Anything else?"

She stirs the pasta and eyes the timer. "You said something about planting, so are you in a tractor making those straight lines in the dirt?"

"I think a field trip to the farm is in order."

The timer goes off. With the hot pads, she takes the pot to the sink and pours the noodles into the strainer. "Do I have to wear my innertube?"

I laugh. "Most definitely, although that's going to give your secret away."

"Maybe they'll think I'm looking for a pool."

"There's always the lake." I nod toward the body of water I've swum in plenty, but I wonder if she'd ever entertain it. She doesn't seem the type.

"I might freeze the baby." She gives me that smile she always does as if I can't figure out that she's joking.

"Making fun of me for being protective?"

She opens the oven and pulls out a dish I didn't even know I had. There're a lot of vegetables in it and an entire bulb of garlic. The stool scrapes the floor as I rise to watch her work.

She takes the garlic, squeezing the now-soft cloves into the mixture. "This is a dish I perfected in Chicago because eating for one isn't all that enjoyable. This is just a bigger batch."

I admire her thin fingers, and the smell of her perfume overrides the smell of the garlic and oil and whatever herbs she has in there. I step closer, my chest hitting her upper arm, but she doesn't step away. This is dangerous territory, but I'm probably the only one thinking that because right now, I'd do about anything to take her upstairs and sink into her, forgetting all the shit with the farm and my brothers. Losing myself in sweet moments with her sounds like bliss right now.

"Oh, the garlic bread!" She steps away from me. "Do you mind getting the tray out while I grab the pasta?"

Did she feel the electricity between us too? Or maybe she just felt the start of my dick growing in my jeans. She's got more sense than me, stepping away because she doesn't need another complication in her life.

I pull out the garlic bread that's done to perfection, and she pours the pasta in the dish from the oven, stirring it around with tongs.

"I got into a fight with my brothers today." I figure talking about what's pissing me off might help cool my libido.

She twirls the pasta in the sauce she made. "Okay, what happened?"

"They always undermine me. Think I can't do anything for myself. The thread on my patience finally broke."

She says nothing, rising on her tiptoes to grab two plates from the cupboard, which I take from her hands and dish out the food she made.

"Thing is, I have this social media account where I've been posting things I've filmed on the farm. I did Jude and Sadie's gender reveal."

"I saw that." She follows me outside to the patio with the basket of garlic bread and our drinks. "Gillian showed it to me. It's amazing what you can do with a horse."

"I'm going to leave that line right there. But thank you."

She laughs, sitting down. With the sun still up, I crank up the umbrella to give us some shade.

"I got a ton of views, so I filmed other content. People started making comments about wanting to come to the ranch. So I pitched the idea of a dude ranch to my brothers and Dad before taking it to the rest of the family."

Why is she so easy to talk to? I never would've thought I could open up to anyone, especially her. But here I am, spilling my guts. If she's surprised, she doesn't show it.

"Those are super popular. I've had clients who have done them."

"See, and most of your clients are wealthy, right?"

She hems and haws. "My private ones were, yeah."

"Well, with Sadie pregnant, Jude wants me to take over more on the ranch, so he won't even consider it. Even though until he was going to become a father, he never thought me worthy or capable of taking on more." I refrain from telling her about the deal I made with Ben. I'm not sure how she'd feel about it.

"Is this what you're working on at night and stuff?"

I twirl my pasta around my fork and bring it to my mouth. My taste buds explode in happiness. "This is so good."

"You're dodging the question," she says.

"No, I just didn't want to forget to compliment you. To answer your question, yeah. I want to carve out my own place on the ranch, and it's not running the day-to-day operations. That's Jude's thing, and he loves it, but I like people. I want to work with people."

She looks up from her plate and smiles. "Tell me more."

And so, for the next hour while we sit on the patio, I tell her everything about what I envision. She listens and asks follow-up questions, and when we call it a night, it's like another jolt of excitement has hit my veins.

Screw my brothers. I'm going to do this. Somehow, I'm going to make this happen.

Chapter Sixteen

BRIAR

"How are the classes going?" Darla asks me.

She's not leisurely talking to guests this morning but waiting for me. My back straightens, and my gut clenches because this is it. Am I being let go? People have tried the yoga class and seem like they enjoyed it, but even I know the attendance has been low.

"They're going well," I say.

She falls in line with me as I walk toward the studio. "Scarlett has started to advertise in Hickory, but we recently got word that Wild Bull Ranch is building a spa." She rolls her eyes. "That boy just loves to push buttons."

"Why would he build a spa, and who is *he*?" I ask.

Darla stops at the kitchen doors. There's no way I can have a big breakfast today. So I take a few steps away as if I'm about to go to the studio.

"Walker Matthews. He's got something to prove, but I'm not sure what. He's Plain Daisy's biggest competition. I think he got word about you and now thinks this is how he'll one-up us."

I remember a Walker hitting on me last year at the Plain

Daisy Ranch ball game, so I'm assuming he's one and the same. I actually drove past Wild Bull Ranch the other day and saw how much it resembled Plain Daisy Ranch.

"Anyway, that lit a fire under Scarlett." She shakes her head. "Nothing gets that girl's engine revving like some good old-fashioned competition."

"I imagine with her job, she's all about making this ranch successful."

Scarlett runs the office for the entire ranch, and I'm pretty sure she's in charge of all the financials, marketing, and everything else.

"Exactly. So, keep at it. I've heard great things. Especially the one you did for women over sixty the other day. Brad and I were downtown this weekend, and everyone kept stopping us and telling how sweet you are and how fun the class was. That they didn't think they could bend like that."

"Oh, I'm glad."

"Yeah, I won't fill you in on the rest. Let's just say you spiced up some bedrooms."

I smile and laugh. "Maybe that should be the marketing line."

She points at me and chuckles. "I'm telling Scarlett that idea." She runs her hand down my arm. "Have a good day. I just wanted to check in with you and let you know we're committed to making this work."

Here I was worried for nothing. Although they might not feel the same once they find out I'm pregnant. Maybe that's when they'll kick my ass to the curb.

"No breakfast today?" she asks as I step farther away from the door.

"I had a big one at home."

Her eyes dip to my stomach and fear grips me, until I see she's following my hand. Shit, I really need to figure out a way to tell everyone.

"Aunt Darla!" Emmett walks out of the dining room with Wren on his shoulders.

He and I share a smile, and although it should feel awkward, he's worming his way into my life.

"Briar." Wren wiggles, and Emmett struggles to get her free before she falls headfirst to the ground.

Once her feet hit the floor, I squat and open my arms, allowing Wren to run into them. Her little arms squeeze me tightly.

"I've missed you," she says.

My eyes sting, but I push back the tears. I barely know this girl. Why am I getting emotional?

"Did Briar eat at home, Emmett?" Darla asks.

I stand, bringing Wren with me, her legs wrapping around my waist.

"Yeah, for sure." Emmett holds his hands out for Wren, but Wren doesn't let go of me.

"Are you two in cahoots now? I thought you hated one another." Darla's gaze shifts from me to Emmett.

"I do. She's got cooties," Emmett says, and Wren laughs.

"Yeah, he drives me crazy," I add, but Darla hears the sarcasm and continues to stare us down.

"Emmett drives everyone crazy." Bennett comes out of the dining room with Wren's backpack and coat in hand. "Time to go."

"Hold on." Wren puts her hands on my cheeks and turns me to look at her. "Will you do my hair?"

"Sure." I lower her to the floor while Bennett digs her hairbrush out of his bag then hands it over.

"Jeez, Danson, you'd think you would figure it out by now," Emmett razzes him.

Bennett gives him a fuck off look.

"Okay, why do you call him Danson? I've been meaning to ask." I run the brush through Wren's hair.

Darla rolls her eyes.

I quickly braid Wren's hair, squatting to be level with her.

"Ever seen the movie *Three Men and a Baby*?" Emmett asks.

"Um… I think a long time ago. That guy from *Friends*, right?"

"Tom Selleck? Yes, Briar." Darla appears offended, sighing. "He was Magnum P.I. as well." She stares off dreamily. Guess the mustache does something for her. "But Ted Danson was the baby's biological father in the movie."

Emmett and Bennett laugh at Darla, and she gives them a look of disgust.

"Danson and Wren live at the boys' house, so we joke that it's like *Three Men and a Baby*."

"Who's the third guy?" I ask, knowing his only male cousins are Bennett and Jensen.

"Jensen's friend, Nash," Emmett says.

"And I'm not a baby," Wren says, sounding annoyed.

"Oh, you all live together. That must be fun." I put the ponytail holder around the end of her braid.

"If you think having three bossy boys telling me what to do is fun." She twists around and furrows her forehead.

I point at the mirror on the wall by reception. "Go check it out."

She runs over, and I stand up straight, feeling a little light-headed when I do. I close my eyes for a moment to gain my bearings. A large body comes alongside me, his arm around my waist, allowing me to use him as support.

"She needs to eat. I told you. Jensen is going to make you a plate." Darla disappears into the kitchen.

Wren comes over and wraps her arms around my legs. "My friends are gonna love it. Last time, they all went home and asked their moms to do their hair like mine." She beams, and it makes me smile.

I don't know anything about Wren's mom, but she's clearly not in the picture if she lives at the guys' house.

"That makes me happy," I say, looking at Bennett and handing him the hairbrush.

"Let's go, Wren, I have a meeting," her dad says.

"What is it that you do?" I haven't asked a lot of questions since being here, I realize.

"He plants flowers and trees," Emmett says.

Bennett laughs. "Do I say you ride a horse and tractor? I'm a landscape architect."

Emmett shrugs. "I'm not into fancy titles. Wouldn't bother me."

Darla comes out with a wrapped-up sandwich in hand. "Breakfast sandwich. You'll love it." She thrusts it my way. "Emmett." Her eyes go from him to my sandwich and back to him.

"I'm on it," he says and gives her a salute.

"Wren, let's go," Bennett says, walking toward the door.

"Can I come over to your house sometime?" Wren asks me.

"It's Emmett's house."

She turns to him.

"Of course," he says.

"Yay!" She skips through the lobby toward the door. "Come on, Dad!"

Bennett shakes his head. "Have a great day, everyone." Then they leave.

"I need to go set up. Thank you, Darla. See you at home, Emmett," I say, walking backward down the hall.

"Home, huh?" Darla's eyelids flutter. "Emmett, make sure she eats that sandwich."

"I guess that means I'm your escort." Emmett comes up alongside me.

"Are you going to force-feed me?"

We walk shoulder to shoulder toward the studio, the sandwich hot in my hand.

"I'll make you a deal," he says. "You eat half, and I eat half."

"Or you eat the whole thing?" I ask, stepping into the studio.

He follows me. "I'm kind of with Darla on this one. You need to eat." His gaze falls to my stomach. "You need nourishment, and so does..." He lets his words die on his lips, thank goodness. I'm paranoid about all the ears around here.

"Can I ask you about Wren's mom?"

"You can ask me anything, but it doesn't mean I'll tell you."

I raise my eyebrows. "That's such a dad thing to say."

He chuckles, taking the sandwich from my hands. He takes half and hands me the other half in the wrapper. "She died."

My stomach lurches. "That's horrible."

He bites his sandwich and eyes mine, so I take a bite. Jensen really is a brilliant chef, and I wonder if he's self-taught or went to school.

"Died during childbirth. Wren never even met her."

I can hear the sorrow in his voice. My stomach twists even further, given my own situation. "That's so horrible. I feel terrible for both of them."

He nods, finishing the last bite of his half of the sandwich. "Wren's just now getting to the age when you start to realize your family is different. I still remember when moms would volunteer at school or for sports. Since my mom never came, my friend asked me when my mom was coming. Dad told me to tell him my mom was in heaven. He asked when she was getting back, like it was a vacation. And I said I didn't know. Death and kids aren't an easy mix."

"So, you don't remember anything about your mom?" I

don't remember mine, and I was older than when Emmett lost his mom. The only mother figure I've ever known is Gillian.

"Sometimes I think I do, but then the same stories about her are told all the time, so am I just remembering that?" He shrugs. "I don't know, but I don't think so."

"My mom left after Koa was born. The difference when someone leaves instead of dies is that no one talks about them at all. It's like they never even existed. I have no memories of her or very many pictures." I take another bite of the sandwich. "But why would I want to know anything about someone who didn't want me anyway?"

He comes over and leans in next to me, wrapping his arm around my shoulders. "Bet you didn't realize how much we had in common. Now finish that sandwich so I can hug you."

"Hug me?" I put the last piece in my mouth.

"Don't act like you don't need one. We just divulged to each other the shit that messed us up. We bonded." He tugs me into his side, but when I don't move, he steps in front of me and, using his finger, forces my chin up to make me look at him.

"I wouldn't say bonded." My excuse is weak, but I do feel as if someone understands a little bit of what it feels like to grow up without a mother. Your mom is supposed to love and nurture you. Give you hugs and kiss your boo-boos. Gillian did her best, but she was a kid herself for the majority of my upbringing.

"Bring it in." His hands run down my arms, and I step into him. At first, I don't wrap my arms around him, but he tightens his arms around me. "Life sucks, but the good thing is that you get to change this baby's path. And you get to feel what it's like to be a mother. And you'll be a great one."

"How can you say that? I didn't have a role model." Finally, I wrap my arms around his waist.

His chest vibrates against mine. "Because you'll be hell-bent on giving your kid everything you didn't get. And I know this kid is going to have love in spades."

I rest my chin on his chest, allowing the wall I put up to crumble. And it feels good to let someone else hold me up, even if it is just for a little bit.

Chapter Seventeen

EMMETT

Since I'm still barely talking to Jude, I decide to go home for lunch.

As I enter, Briar is coming down the stairs. She's wearing a white dress that lands right above her knee, showcasing her amazing, toned legs. She's almost always in yoga pants, so rarely do I get to see her legs. They're lean and strong and could probably support her without my help if she were wrapped around my waist as I drilled into her.

"You're not usually home this early," she says, putting an earring in one ear.

"Lunch."

"There's that chicken casserole I made that you could heat up."

"Thanks, wifey." I open the fridge to cool myself down after looking at her.

"Whenever you get married, do not call your wife wifey."

I peek my head out of the fridge. She has her laptop open in front of her. "It was a joke."

"I know, I'm just giving you some advice." She sits at my

kitchen table, staring at the screen as if it makes her nervous or something.

"Don't worry, I plan on calling my wife bitch. Or maybe broad." I pull out the leftovers and grab a plate.

She shakes her head and gives me no comeback, which makes me frown.

"What are you looking at?" I spoon the leftovers onto the plate.

She leans back in the chair and looks at me. "Just checking out the OBGYN doctors in the area."

Fuck, I hadn't even thought about that. Has she even been to see an actual doctor yet?

"Oh."

She nods. "Yeah, oh. I need to find one, and I can't see one in Willowbrook. Even Hickory is too close. I haven't told Gillian yet, and she can't find out from some stranger."

"There's always Lincoln."

It's about forty-five minutes away, which isn't crazy, but when she goes into labor, I'm sure she doesn't want a forty-five-minute drive to the hospital.

"I think it's my only choice."

I put my dish in the microwave and start it, then sit at the table with her. "Why haven't you told Gillian yet, if you don't mind me asking?"

"Because I should've learned my lesson from what happened to her."

"Your situation is completely different. You trusted someone, and he broke that. You're not a fool, and I'm sure Gillian won't see it that way."

She fiddles with the piece of paper. "I'll still be disappointing her, and she's done so much for me. She'll think I ruined my life." Her eyes flood with tears.

I have no idea how to navigate this situation. "I think

you're wrong, but that's just my opinion." The microwave beeps off, and I stand to get my lunch.

"Will you come with me?" she asks.

Thank God my back is to her because I'm sure the look on my face reads pure terror. "Um..."

"I don't want to go by myself, and I have no one else to ask."

I bring my plate to the table and eat a few bites before I answer. I've been happy to help her through this thus far, but I'm starting to feel attached. To take her to the doctor and to talk about her being pregnant... I need to sever this tie that feels as though it's binding us, rather than cranking up the tension on it. Lately I've been looking forward to coming home at night and running into her at The Getaway Lodge. My mind is always searching through ways to make her smile or get her through this stressful time in her life.

"Never mind. I can go myself." She stands from the table, taking the paper and phone.

I grab her wrist, running my thumb along the inside, feeling her soft skin. "I'll go. Just tell me when, and I'll get it off."

"You don't have to."

I know I don't, but I want to be there for her since no one else can be right now. I fork another heaping bite of the chicken casserole. "Just say thank you, Briar."

"Thank you."

I release her wrist, and my mind floats to an image of pulling her into my lap, telling her I'll take her to any doctor's appointment she wants. Hell, I'll do everything I can to make this easier for her.

"I had an idea I wanted to run by you." She sits back down, crossing her legs, and my eyes drift to the side of the table where her shapely legs are on display.

My hand tightens on the fork. All of these little signs are not good. Finding her attractive and wanting her is one thing. But I'm worried about wanting to help her, fix the situation, take the weight off her shoulders. I've seen my brothers do that with Gillian and Sadie. It means there's more than your dick involved.

"An idea?" I ask, concentrating on my plate, not allowing my gaze to veer to her legs.

"I'll film you. I was on your account, and I have some ideas for videos I think might get you even more views."

"Like?" I still don't look over at her. Suddenly this chicken casserole is the most interesting thing I've seen all week.

"Well, I'm thinking we should do something by the lake. And that horseshoe fitting one was great, but we could tweak it a little the next time you have to do it. And everyone loved you at the gender reveal, so we should offer those, too."

I ignore the way her words make my chest warm. "Okay," I say down to my plate.

"The more followers you get, the more you'll show your family how seriously you're taking this and what a good opportunity it is. You know, I was talking to Darla, and she mentioned some Walker guy is opening a spa?"

My gut twists. Is Briar thinking about working for our rival?

"He's an asshole," I say, hoping it deters her if that's the case.

"That's why if he gets any idea about what you want to do, he's going to double down, so we need to make sure he can't reach you even if he tries."

I finally look up at her. She has a point. Walker likes to compete with us, but really, he copies us. Opening a spa after we offer yoga classes? He's already building a lodge but playing it off as a bed-and-breakfast with some cute name I can't remember.

"Let's meet here right after you get off." She smiles and does an excited dance in her seat. "I'm going to do more research."

I nod, and she gets up and walks away. I finish my lunch, rinse the plate, and put it in the dishwasher. I'm not sure I want to know what she has in mind.

Chapter Eighteen

BRIAR

"You want me to do what?" Emmett asks, staring at the lake.

"What you usually do in the lake." I have my phone out, ready to take a video.

"I skinny dip." His tone is so serious, I can't contain my laugh.

"Skinny dip?"

"Yes."

"With someone?"

He grins. "Wouldn't you like to know?"

"No, I really wouldn't."

I smother my urge to ask more questions. Whoever he skinny dips with, they're lucky. Since I started living with him, I've not only forgiven Emmett for what he did in high school, but I find myself attracted to him for more than his looks. Which I shouldn't be. Not that anyone could blame me for wanting the man. I'm pretty sure he doesn't walk into a room without all eyes following him. But I'm pregnant with another man's baby. I'm off a recent break-up that crushed me. So this pull toward Emmett isn't something I can entertain.

He narrows his eyes and smirks as if he can read my mind.

"Get in there and cool off after a hard day at the ranch. You're kind of dirty today, so that'll work."

"You want me to go in there fully clothed?" He looks at the lake and back at me.

"Yes. Then you're going to take your shirt off."

"Whoa, whoa, whoa. You trying to make me into a sex symbol?"

"As if you'd mind." I hold up my phone. "We're simply showing how you cool down on the ranch. If someone sees it as sexual, then that's on them."

"Way to twist it." He walks around me and onto the small dock. "Want me to just fall in on my back? Dive? What will it be, director?"

I rock my head side to side. "I love both ideas." Both are sexy, I think.

"I'll fall on my back like I'm exhausted. Then I'll swim to where it's waist deep and take off my shirt."

"Who's the director now?"

"I'm just helping you sell me. Obviously you think I'm sexy." Why does that knowing smile make my insides flutter?

"All right, I'm going to do the three-finger countdown, then do it. We only have one take since you have to be dry. And leave the cowboy hat on."

He takes it off. "Hell no, then I'll have to wait for it to dry to wear it again."

I wave the phone. "Do you want the views?"

"Fine." He turns around so his back is to the water.

The sun is descending, shining down on him, casting a shadow over his beautiful face. God, he's sexy.

I hold up my hand, counting down from three to one. As soon as I have one finger up, he flawlessly falls back into the water. There's a big splash around him as he sinks down.

Then he pops up, grabs his hat, and swims over to the edge

where I am. He stands where it's waist deep and unsnaps his plaid shirt. He couldn't have picked a better outfit to wear. His chest glistens, his abs so firm and defined that my fingers itch to run down them like the droplets of water are currently doing. Then he puts his cowboy hat back on, and I have to squeeze my legs together.

"Nothing better than a dip in the lake after a hard day's work. Come on down to Plain Daisy Ranch," he says right into the camera.

I click to end the recording. "It's scary how good you were."

"I do love to entertain people." He walks toward the edge of the deck. "Let me see."

I step closer, holding the phone out to him.

"Closer," he says.

"Emmett, I can't come any closer without getting in."

He wraps his arm around my waist, plucking my phone out of my hand and tossing it over onto the grassy bank.

"Don't you dare!"

"What?" he says, but we both know what he's about to do.

"Emmett!" I shout right before he falls backward, taking me with him.

The water is cool, way cooler than I'm sure it is during the summer. It's only the end of April.

"Holy shit, it's freezing." I stomp out of the water, covering my body.

He's laughing and swimming to get his cowboy hat, then he walks up out of the water. I wish I had the video going then. Any woman would be drooling over him.

"I'll make it up to you," he says, stripping his shirt completely off and wrapping his arms around my waist, picking me up and drawing me to him. He shakes his hair and water droplets ping along my skin.

"Stop." I laugh and push against his chest, and he lowers my feet to the ground. As I slide down his body, my nipples feel every ridge of his muscular chest. This was a very bad idea.

My feet hit the grass, but neither one of us steps back.

"You're a jerk," I say, trying to break up the awkwardness of this moment.

"Oh, come on. It was fun." His eyes land on mine, and he raises his hand. I think he's going to cradle my cheek, but his fingers stop on my shoulder, pushing the strap of my dress back up. "How about a hot bath?"

I stare up at him, and my gaze falls to his lips.

What kind of kisser is Emmett Noughton? I don't see him as cautious; rather, he probably takes what he wants, putting every emotion into the kiss.

Both our breathing picks up, and it feels as if some invisible force is pulling us closer together. I inch up on my toes, and he bends his head down, sliding his hand to the back of my head.

"Emmett," I whisper, and I'm not even sure why. To stop this foolishness, or give him permission?

"Tell me," he says, his strong fingers weaving through my strands, tilting my head back.

Kiss me are the two words I want to say. Kiss me until my lips tingle and my core clenches.

But I can't make another bad decision for myself. I pull back right before his lips land on mine. "I'm freezing," I lie because I was warm in his arms.

He releases me and stops, staring at my chest.

"What?" I ask, looking down to see how very see-through my white dress now is. You can clearly see my nipples through my white dress and sheer bra. I wrap an arm around my chest and one between my legs. "Well, there you go. You've practically seen me naked now."

"Not even close," he says.

There's a drawl in his voice that confirms he was feeling what I was feeling with that almost kiss. We were so close to breaking past that barrier, but I was smart enough to pull away before we got in over our heads. Proof, I guess, that I don't only make bad decisions.

Chapter Nineteen

BRIAR

We walk into the doctor's office, and I realize right away that all the other women are way further along in their pregnancies than I am. Most women's hands are wrapped around their swollen bellies, or they're reading magazines resting on their stomachs.

I go up to the receptionist while Emmett stands at my back. The young girl's eyes go to Emmett before landing on me.

"Hi, how can I help you?" She's a cute brunette with a friendly smile.

"Briar Adams. I have an appointment."

She flips through some folders. "New patient, right?"

"Yeah."

"I just need you to fill this out. Medical history, insurance information, emergency contact."

I clench my fist to stop my hand from shaking before accepting the clipboard. "Great, thanks."

"Have a seat. They'll call you in when they're ready." She signals with her hand to the waiting room.

Emmett waits for me to pick a seat. I'm usually careful and

sit away from people. I don't care for people who want to chat up everyone in the waiting room and ask questions about their lives, so I steer clear of them. I sit in the corner, and Emmett sits beside me, manspreading so his thigh is touching mine. I'm not sure why, but I find it comforting.

I start filling out the form. "Um, Emmett..." I whisper.

"Yeah?"

"The second question is my address."

He shrugs. "Put mine."

"But—"

"Just put mine."

With so much online these days, I haven't had to think much about the change of my address.

"If you're sure."

"I'm sure." He nods toward the clipboard.

I fill out all the information I have, digging out my insurance card from Plain Daisy Ranch. Of course they would offer their part-time employees health benefits. They might regret it when they find out I'm pregnant if their benefits package goes up. Then I stare at the Emergency Contact box. Huh. It would usually be Gillian, and I could put her. I mean, what are the chances something happens to me?

Emmett grabs the clipboard then snatches the pen, scribbling his name and phone number on the form, then hands it back to me.

"Thanks?" I say-slash-ask. My heart skips a beat that he's being so kind about this situation. Especially since I feel like a loser. Everything in my life is up in the air, and I'm about to bring another being into the world.

"I'm your person." He doesn't face me, instead staring forward. "You know, until Gillian knows."

"Definitely." That hard thing inside me softens a little more.

He taps his fingers on his thigh. A habit I've noticed he has whenever he's uncomfortable. Does being alone with me make him uncomfortable? When I first moved in, I felt that way, but now he's almost like a friend.

When I hear his headboard hit my wall at night when he gets into bed, comfort washes over me because he feels near. It's so stupid. I should still hate the man. Hell, I shouldn't want any man in my life right now. But Emmett is gentle and patient with me, and those are my turn-ons. I do love his cocky side and the way he makes me laugh. He's sexy, but this softer side he's showing me is something I could grow to love if I don't stop myself.

"Excuse me." A woman comes to stand in front of Emmett, one hand resting on her swollen stomach. If I had to guess, I'd say she's about halfway through her pregnancy. "Are you that guy from Plain Daisy Ranch?"

My eyebrows shoot up, and I whip my head to the side to look at Emmett. He raises his head, looking my way before circling back to her.

"He is," I answer, way more excited than I probably should be.

"I see your videos on socials. I keep telling my husband I want to come down and check it out." She sits in the chair across from Emmett. "Do you hire out for the gender reveal parties?"

Emmett chuckles and side-eyes me. "That was for my brother."

"Yeah, I read that. Congratulations to them. I haven't had my gender reveal yet because I want something unique. That's what drove me to your videos. Would you consider doing mine?"

"Um..." Emmett shifts in his seat.

"Excuse my manners. My name is Parker." She holds out her hand.

"Emmett." He shakes it, and she moves her hand to me.

Parker looks at me with a sigh. "I don't even remember what it was like to have a flat tummy anymore. Then again, it was never as flat as yours." She eyes my stomach.

I politely smile and cover it up with the ends of my cardigan. "Good to meet you, I'm Briar."

"What a pretty name. Emmett and Briar. Those names are written in the stars because you two are so darn cute. How far along are you?"

"Oh, um..." I start to tell her that Emmett isn't the dad, but he links his hand with mine. A warm, buzzing sensation travels up my arm.

"It's still early, but I can't wait to watch her stomach swell with our baby."

I force myself to smile at Emmett. He really can be a great salesman.

"Now I see why my husband's been pushing off the idea of you doing the gender reveal. He's probably afraid you'll steal my heart like you did hers." Her gaze flickers back and forth, her smile widening as she sits across from us.

"Aw, you got it all wrong. She stole mine." Emmett squeezes my hand.

I cough and clear my throat, causing Emmett to smirk, but he gives nothing away. I have to remind myself that nothing he's saying is true. He's just playing some game. Either that or making it so I don't have to confess how messed up my situation is to a perfect stranger.

Parker leans back in her seat. "Did you hear that, ladies? Briar here scored herself a *real* man. And he's a cowboy."

The other women in the waiting room give her polite smiles, and their eyes fall to our joined hands. His calluses are rough, and his hand is huge, swallowing mine, but the way he runs his thumb along the edge of my pointer finger... Jesus, he might as well be running it over my clit.

"So? Can I hire you?" Parker asks.

"Yeah, I just did that for my brother. We don't officially—"

"We could come to you," she says. "I was going to make it a closed affair anyway. Then we'll record it for everyone else to see. We could stay on the grounds, or is there other lodging nearby? I looked it up, and it's only forty-five minutes away, right?"

Holy shit, how much digging has she done?

"I'd have to check the schedule."

I lean forward. "I'm sure we could manage it. We'd have to check with the lodge where I teach yoga classes."

"Pregnancy ones?" she asks, her eyes lighting up.

"Yes, I mean obviously, since I am pregnant as well."

Emmett chuckles, amused because I'm now selling the idea.

"And there's a winery and a flower farm and this cute store..."

Parker takes out her phone.

"Look up their website. I'm sure we could get a package together for you." I'm lying through my teeth, but this woman is dressed like a lot of my old clients. No doubt her husband works in some executive tower. They probably have rich friends.

"My husband, God help him, acts like he could do what you do on a horse." She frantically swipes on her phone.

"I could teach him. We've been thinking about starting a dude ranch," Emmett says.

"His daddy shower! That's perfect." She grins at us.

"I'm sorry?" I've never heard that term before.

"I promised him a trip before the new baby comes. Like a bachelor party but before the baby comes. They were talking Vegas. What's with Vegas?" She looks at Emmett.

He's still blinking. I think he believes it's as absurd as I do, but who knows? The person I thought Emmett was would love any excuse for a guys' trip.

When neither of us says anything, she continues. "I get one after. My girlfriends are taking me to Bora Bora. You know, after I get the nanny all up to speed. This is our fourth, so we'll probably have to hire a second one to help handle our brood. Hold on." She digs in her purse, taking a receipt out and a pen. "Please call me or email me. I really want to make this happen."

I take the piece of paper from her. "We'll definitely be in touch."

She does a soft clap and wiggles in her seat.

The nurse peeks her head out of the door. "Briar Adams."

"She's right here!" Parker points at me.

I stand with my clipboard, unfortunately letting go of Emmett's hand.

"Don't forget hubby," Parker says.

I stop a few feet away, holding out my hand to Emmett, not bothering to correct her. She already thinks Emmett is the dad, so what's the point? If she does end up doing something with the ranch, I'll just tell her we eloped and to please not mention it to anyone on the ranch or something.

"Oh yeah, hubby, come on." I look at Parker with a smile. "And they say only women have pregnancy brain."

"Wifey, I thought I was going to stay out here." Emmett glances nervously between Parker and me.

"No, silly, you come in too."

"Are you sure?" Emmett asks.

I lock eyes with Emmett, hoping he sees that he needs to sell this. "No, I want my guy next to me the whole time," I say in a baby voice.

I smile at Parker who looks over the moon as though she just met a celebrity. I tug and he finally follows me toward the door.

"Mr. and Mrs. Adams, right this way."

"Noughton!" Parker calls. "That's your last name, right?"

"I'm really scared right now," Emmett whispers.

"Oh, yeah, independent woman not wanting to take her husband's last name." I wave my hand like I'm crazy, right?

"Good for you. Talk to you soon." She waves.

Thankfully the door shuts, but Emmett is white as a ghost.

The nurse weighs me and measures my height. After she leaves the room to wait for the doctor, Emmett scootches to the end of his chair.

"Am I going to see…" His eyes shift to between my legs.

"Well, yeah," I say, just to mess with him. "You said you're my person. I thought you'd be my Lamaze partner and be there for the birth too." I pretend to be upset, and Emmett's face falls.

Yeah, I'm gonna let him sweat it out a little until the doctor comes in.

Chapter Twenty

EMMETT

Briar twirls her finger in the air. "Turn around, I have to take my pants off."

Briar has accomplished something not many have before her—she's silenced me. I have no idea what to say.

"This isn't how I imagined the first time I'd see your pussy." I turn to face the wall and stare at a poster that showcases all the stages of pregnancy.

"How did you imagine you'd first see my vagina?"

"With my head between your thighs." I love the fact she didn't squirm and asked a question in response. Briar can always give as good as she gets.

"Want to do your worst before the doctor comes in?" I hear the rustling of the paper sheet the nurse gave her. "There're stirrups and everything."

"You're tempting me to prove to you that I'll do it."

"You can turn around." When I do, she's sitting on the edge of the bed with the paper sheet over her. This is a lot harder than I imagined. "Eyes up here."

"You have no idea the control this is taking me."

She laughs. "You act as if we're actually together, and I give you access to my body whenever you want."

A man can dream, right?

Before I can come back with a witty remark, there's a knock on the door. "All ready, Briar?"

"Yes." She points at me to sit back down.

I do so like an obedient dog because I have no fucking clue how I'm going to get out of this appointment without a red face and saying something inappropriate.

A doctor with a white jacket comes in and eyes me first, then Briar. She shakes Briar's hand. "I'm Dr. Morales."

"Hi. This is Emmett." She thumbs my way.

I put out my hand. "Nice to meet you."

"Well, you're the talk of the waiting room." She goes to the sink and washes her hands. "Parker outed you." She laughs.

"Yeah, we met her," I say, still unsure what to think about that interaction.

"I think everyone did. She's a lovely woman."

"And persistent," Briar says.

Dr. Morales wipes her hands with the paper towels and tosses them in a trash can. "That she is." She sits on the stool in front of the computer, scanning her badge to unlock it. "So, you're pregnant?"

Briar nods.

"Did this happen naturally or through fertility treatments?"

"Naturally. It was a surprise." Briar cringes.

Dr. Morales stares at her as though she doesn't understand Briar's reaction.

"We weren't going to try so soon," I say, hoping to lead her away from the truth of the situation and the fact that I'm not the father.

"Well, a baby is a great surprise, but having four of my

own, I can say that even when you plan it, you're never quite ready." She turns to Briar. "Do you remember the first day of your last period?"

I shouldn't be here for this conversation. This is not a pretend husband's place, but I guess if I'm pretending, then I should be here. My brain is so scrambled right now, wondering how the hell I've found myself in this position.

Because you're a nurturer, and Briar needs a reliable person right now.

What she doesn't need is a dick, especially my dick in her pussy.

Briar answers all her questions. Dr. Morales is very nice and what I'd imagine a doctor who delivers babies would be like.

"I'd like to do an ultrasound to make sure the positioning is good in the womb. We might even be able to hear the heart-beat depending on how far along you are."

Briar's head whips toward me with shock. Are we ready for that step? No. No, we're not. Gillian should be here to hold Briar's hand. Hell, asshat should really be here, but he's too busy raising his other kids and cheating on his wife.

"Lie down," Dr. Morales instructs, and Briar's back falls to the table.

Then Dr. Morales pulls out the stirrups and gently guides Briar's heels to rest in them.

I'm trying not to look, but how can I not? This is the weirdest situation I've ever been in. A girl I'm attracted to is lying on a table with her legs in stirrups, about to have a pelvic exam.

"Just relax. It won't take long." Dr. Morales ducks under the sheet, her stool sliding along the floor.

"You're where I like to be," I say.

Briar's mouth hangs open, and her eyes bore into mine.

Dr. Morales peeks out, laughing. "That's not one I've heard before."

"Really? It felt a little lame, but I tend to make jokes in awkward—"

"Why don't you come hold my hand, hubby?" Briar holds out her hand toward me with a "shut up" expression on her face.

I walk over to her. I slide my hand into hers, and she squeezes so tightly, my knees almost buckle. Doesn't she know this is only gonna fuel me to embarrass her more?

"Can we take one of these paper gowns home?" I ask. "We like to role play."

"He's joking," Briar shoots me the death stare I used to get from her before she moved in.

Dr. Morales comes out from between her legs. Another person that gets to see how pretty Briar's pussy is.

"Now I see why you're such a sensation in your videos." She slides back and takes off her gloves, standing and disposing of them in the trash. Dr. Morales goes over to a machine. "Since I think you're barely ten weeks, I'm going to do a transvaginal ultrasound, if that's okay?"

"What does that mean?" I ask, and Dr. Morales laughs.

"Sure, it's fine." Another glare from Briar on the bed.

She's the one who demanded I come in here. I was willing to wait with my new bff in the waiting room.

Dr. Morales turns off the lights.

"Mood lighting, I like it," I say.

Dr. Morales laughs again, enjoying my jokes, but Briar keeps trying to break my fingers with her squeezes.

"Please excuse him, he's practicing his dad jokes for when this little guy or girl is twelve."

Dr. Morales goes to the ultrasound machine and takes out what looks like a huge-ass dildo.

"Whoa, you're making me insecure now," I say.

"Seriously?" Briar turns to me. "Sorry again," she says to Dr. Morales.

"This one usually makes the men a little uneasy, but don't look at it as competition." She laughs at her own joke and earns a giggle from Briar.

"I'm never jealous. I know how to satisfy—" My words stop when I watch her put what looks like a condom and lube on the wand. "You're going to..."

She takes it out of the holder. "Would you like to guide it, Briar, or do you want me to?"

I raise my hand. "Can I do it?"

"This isn't a game at the fair," Briar says. "You can do it, Dr. Morales."

The wand disappears under the sheet, and I watch Briar for a reaction to having something so long inside her. Based on her lack of a response, she could definitely handle me. Yeah, that one was lame.

Then the screen is all black and white, and Briar's head turns to watch as Dr. Morales does whatever she does.

"I'd say you're about eleven weeks," Dr. Morales says.

"Really? I swore—"

"We can never tell the exact date of conception if you're very sexually active. But everything looks really good." She touches the screen, and a whooshing sound comes out of the monitor. "Let's get this little one's heartbeat, shall we?" I see her hand moving under the sheet, then a fast heartbeat sounds throughout the room. "There we go."

It all seems so real now that I can hear the baby inside her.

Briar watches intently, tears slipping down her cheeks onto the paper sheet. "It's so fast."

"That's normal. Your little one looks perfect. I'm going to take a few pictures for you to take with you. Congratulations to you both."

The heartbeat sound stops, but I still stare at the screen, unsure what to say.

Dr. Morales glances at me and laughs. "Dads always get a little edgy at the first ultrasound. They get nervous that it's all real, and they're going to have another one to take care of."

Briar looks at me. "Are you okay?"

I swallow past the golf ball-sized lump in my throat. "Yeah. Of course."

I mean, the baby isn't mine. But it's so fragile and innocent, growing in Briar's stomach. How do I already feel such an attachment just from hearing the heartbeat? Just from being there for its mother?

"Okay, I'll let you get dressed," Dr. Morales says. "Make an appointment in a month from now. I'll give you a prescription for prenatal vitamins. If anything happens that's unusual, you call. I saw you're from Willowbrook. I'm happy to be your doctor, but would you like if I partnered with a physician closer to you in case—"

"No!" Briar practically shouts. No, she's not acting suspicious at all. "We're happy to drive up here. Thank you, though."

Dr. Morales nods and points at me. "I'm hoping for a fresh set of jokes on the next visit. I like you." She smiles at both of us and walks out the door.

Briar steps down from the table. "What's with the jokes?" She tries to wrap the paper sheet around her waist, but it tears. She scrambles to fix it.

"She liked my jokes."

"Turn around," she says, twirling her finger.

I hear the crumpling of the sheet and her sighing.

"Come on. They were funny."

"Maybe a little bit." She comes to my side, fully dressed. "Ready?"

"You don't have to ask twice. It felt like a torture chamber in here." I open the door for her.

"You weren't the one with her legs spread and a giant dildo thing inside her." She walks past me toward reception.

"That doesn't sound so bad if you're a woman."

She stops and turns to me. "Then next time, we'll stick the wand up your ass. Tell me how comfortable that is."

I hold up my hands. "I meant torture chamber because your pussy was right there, and I couldn't even take a peek or a lick."

Her face flushes, and it's the cutest thing.

"You're thinking about my face between your legs, aren't you?"

"No." She spins around.

"You so are." I grin.

She ignores me and makes her next appointment with a red face.

Yeah, I think Briar Adams might like me if even just a little. And I shouldn't like that fact as much as I do.

Chapter Twenty-One

BRIAR

"I don't think I'm going to go," I say from where I sit on the couch with the remote in my hand.

All of the cousins and friends are meeting at The Hidden Cave tonight—the local dive bar. Gillian has already asked me ten times if I'm going.

Emmett plops down on the couch next to me. "That's cool, I'll stay in with you. Want to watch a movie?"

I swivel in his direction. "You go. I'm fine."

"Why don't you want to go?"

"Because I can't not drink without someone asking questions."

"Tell them you're in recovery."

I kick him. "That's not funny, and Gillian already gave me a questioning look at Sunday dinner again when I said I didn't want wine. I used to drink casually more often."

He stands and holds out his hand. "Let me take care of it."

"How are you going to take care of it?" I wrap the blanket around my lap tighter, settling in for the night.

"Trust me. I'm your Lamaze partner. If you trust me with your birth, you can trust me to make everyone think you're drinking when you're not." He inches his open palm toward me.

"The Lamaze partner thing was a joke. I'm sure I'll gain the courage to tell Gillian by then." Although that feels like a lie at the moment. I've tried a few times to tell her and always end up chickening out. If Dr. Morales is right, and I'm eleven weeks, I don't have a ton of time left before I'm showing.

"Come on." Emmett ignores my comment, not letting his hand fall. "I promise a good time."

I accept his hand, and he pulls me up. Truth is, I would love to have a fun night out with everyone, most especially Emmett. Which is a problem. A big one. But lately I find myself wanting to spend time with him.

"There you go. Now go get all pretty."

I quirk an eyebrow.

"Not that you're not gorgeous and hot as fuck just sitting on the couch like you were."

I shake my head and walk toward the stairs. "Are you gonna ditch me for some woman tonight?" I turn at the bottom of the stairs and look at him.

"I can only handle one woman in my life at a time. You're it right now, sweetheart." He winks, and I realize he hasn't done that in a while. It fills my stomach with flutters and excitement—a very bad sign.

He climbs the steps behind me, and we both disappear into our bedrooms. I hear his shower turn on, and my mind floods with images of his fit, naked body under the hot spray—pellets of water slipping down his tanned skin and rippling muscles.

I lie down on my bed, imagining him sliding his hand down to his hardening length because he's thinking of me. Thinking of doing things to me, things he shouldn't. Unspeakable things, but he can't control himself.

My hand slides under the waist of my lounge pants,

pushing past the elastic barrier of my underwear. My finger drifts through my wetness, and I circle my clit, bringing the other hand up to tweak my sensitive nipple. All the sexual tension of living with Emmett after years of having a crush on him rises to the surface. I need this. It's been too long since I've made myself come because my mind has been occupied with more important things.

But I can't stop myself.

In my mind, I'm in the shower with Emmett, and those rough ranch hands are skimming up my body, molding to my swollen tits while his thumbs run over my nipples. I arch my back, offering him everything he's willing to take.

"These tits. You've been driving me crazy." His voice is husky without an ounce of restraint.

He bends, pushing my tits together, sucking one nipple into his mouth before moving to the other one. I watch him, my core clenching, aching for him to be inside me.

"Oh god." My back arches and Emmett takes the opportunity to press me into the tiled wall, his lips casting kisses up my skin to my mouth.

"I've waited so long to have you," he says before his lips crash to mine.

Our tongues tangle, discovering each other. His knuckles drag down the side of my ribcage, and he lifts my leg to his hip, grinding his length against my core. I use my strength to bring my other leg up, and his hands grip my ass.

"Fuck me, Emmett."

I anchor my arms around his neck, and he slides into me, both of us groaning from having what we've wanted for so long. All those long, admiring stares, wondering what it would feel like to be together, come down to this moment.

"You're so wet," he says into my neck, repositioning me so he can get deeper.

"Take what you want," I say. "I'm yours."

He draws his head back. "Hell yeah, you are. Remember that."

His declaration wraps me in a cocoon, and it's only him and me, conquering the world hand in hand. He pulls out and pushes inside me again.

On the bed, my fingers plunge into my pussy, imagining it's him, I'm sure, impressive length and girth stretching me.

"Harder," I tell him in my mind, and he drives into me, spreading my ass cheeks and tugging me in at the same time.

Over and over again he takes me. He doesn't relent. I grasp on to keep hold, my orgasm barreling forward like a semi with the brakes out.

"Fuck, Briar. You're perfect," he pants in my ear, his labored breaths causing a wake of goose bumps along my flesh.

My insides clench in both real life and my imagination. I lock my arms around his neck to anchor myself to him. Every muscle in my body seizes right before stars explode behind my eyes.

"Oh god, Emmett." I let myself enjoy having something I've wanted for so long.

"Shit, you're beautiful when you come."

My fingers weave through his wet hair, and he pushes me against the wall again, holding me steady. I let him take me how he needs me, and soon, he stills inside me, his hard body pressing against mine. I feel his dick twitch as he pours into me.

"What have you done to me?" he whispers.

I smile. The teenage girl inside me is happy she finally got what she wanted.

A knock sounds on the door, and I pull my hand out from under my pants, panic flaring to life.

"I'll be downstairs waiting," Emmett says, and I hear his footsteps jog down the hardwood stairs a second later.

Oh, this is so bad. So fucking bad.

I sit up in bed, rehashing what I just did. I masturbated to images of Emmett fucking me in the shower. I shake my head as if that will make the vision I expertly manifested vanish.

My body is hot, my core not close to satisfied with my hand. If anything, I'm even more aroused, and there's only one man who can douse the flames. A man who's known for not caring much for responsibility or for being reliable. A man who is not the father of the baby I'm carrying. A man who is my roommate and my sister's future-brother-in-law.

I'm so screwed.

Chapter Twenty-Two

EMMETT

We walk into The Hidden Cave, and since it's a nice night, we find everyone hanging out on the outside patio. There's a stage for live bands, rows of picnic tables, and the bar is an old silo they cut down and put a bar top on, then added a roof. There are no waitresses going to the picnic tables. It's a come-and-get-it place, which is perfect for the situation we're in tonight.

My hand itches to grab Briar's hand, but I slide it into my jeans pocket instead. She wouldn't be happy to draw attention to the fact that we've become friends and become more affectionate with one another. If we pass one another in the kitchen, usually a hand touches a shoulder or a back to let the other person know we're passing behind them. The other night, she fell asleep on me while watching some reality television show she said she loves. I should've woken her up or propped a pillow under her head, but instead I let her lie on my shoulder.

"Briar!" Gillian raises her hand and beelines it over to us. She wraps her arms around her sister. She pulls away and studies her. "Have you been dodging me?"

"Hey, Gilly Bean," I say to distract her, but she gives me a fleeting glance and concentrates back on Briar.

"No, I've just been busy," Briar says.

Gillian looks at her skeptically, grabs her hand, and drags her over to the girls' table.

"Good to see you, Gilly Bean. Chat later? Okay." I wave my hand at her back.

Briar shoots me a pleading look over her shoulder.

"I'll get you a drink. Margarita?" I say loudly enough for everyone to hear me.

Briar smiles, but it's not the one I'm used to seeing lately. It's forced and etched with worry.

I head over to the bar. "Hey, Tammy," I say to the blonde bartender as she places a napkin down for me.

I smack Melvin, the owner's son, who has a designated stool right next to the outdoor version of The Canary Wall, Willowbrook's biggest gossip board. He says he likes the spot, but I think it's to make sure no one pulls the notecards off the board if the gossip is about them. There's only one person who Melvin didn't say anything to once, and that was Jude.

I let Tammy know I'm going to chat with Melvin for a second and that she can go on and help another customer.

"Emmett, where the hell have you been lately?" Melvin asks, with good reason.

The Hidden Cave was my regular Saturday night place until Briar moved in. I came a few times after she moved in, but I started to feel weird leaving her on the couch to go find pussy.

"Busy. Jude's teaching me the lay of the land."

He nods and sips his beer. The man has the tolerance of a bull.

"Do you mind if I make myself a drink?" I ask, not sure what he'll say. But Tammy is close to Gillian, and if I order a non-alcoholic drink for Briar, she might casually mention something to Gillian. Nothing is safe in our small town.

"Why you wanna make your own?"

I lean in close to his ear, looking around the space. "I'm trying to impress someone, and she has a favorite drink that I'm trying to replicate for her. You know, it'll help me score some points." I pull back, and Melvin laughs.

"You found someone you want to put effort into impressing?"

His humor is warranted. I've never really cared that much about any of the girls I've either hooked up with or dated.

Now that I think about it, I'm doing so much for Briar, and I'm not getting anything in return. I'm not even expecting or really hoping for anything, given the situation she's in.

Shit, that's a realization I hadn't had before.

"Have at it." Melvin motions toward the bar. "Tammy, Emmett's coming back."

"Good, he can help me with his obnoxious cousins." She doesn't seem bothered, which is good.

"Thanks, man." I pat Melvin on the back and round the edge of the bar.

Usually, I'm boisterous, asking who needs a drink, but I need to do this on the sly. My eyes are trained on Gillian and my cousins to make sure no one sees me. Thanks to the internet, I found a recipe for a Margarita Mocktail and memorized it while waiting for Briar to get ready.

Do not think about what happened before you came here.

I keep the glass low, pouring juices and sparkling water into a margarita glass. I put salt around the rim and add a lime. Pretty damn good if you ask me.

Grabbing myself a beer, I nod a thanks to Melvin and step out from behind the bar.

"Already done?" Tammy asks, eyeing my drinks. She was way too slammed to have noticed how I made the drink.

"Don't worry, I'll be back." I wink, and she rolls her eyes.

My female cousins and their friends sit at a picnic table while all the guys sit at a high table off to the side. I haven't really talked to Jude or Ben since our fight. I take Jude's instruction when he gives it, and I'm thankful he's a quiet guy who doesn't like discussing feelings. So I don't expect him to actually apologize or talk to me about what went down. We'll do what we mostly always do—brush it under the rug and move on.

I set the drink in front of Briar, and immediately all my cousins' attention falls on me.

"You got Briar a drink?" Lottie asks.

"Jealous?" I ask.

"That's gross. I'm your cousin. Never say that again." Lottie sips her usual frozen drink from the machines The Hidden Cave invested in a couple of years ago.

"I guess if my name was Brooks, it'd be a different story."

Her jaw twists, and she narrows her eyes. "Go hang with the boys." She shoos me with her hand.

"You sure? Brooks is over there. Should I ask him if he has his handcuffs on him?"

"He's like a brother to me." Lottie tries to blow it off, but I'm certain there's something between those two. The question is whether they've figured it out yet or not.

Gillian disregards me and turns to Briar. "So, is it horrible living with him?"

Briar looks up at me with an expression of save me, but the rest of the table looks at me like when are you going to fucking leave. I'm tempted to sit my ass down just to annoy them further.

"Thanks for the drink," Briar says.

Gillian's head rears back, staring at Briar as if she had said she was pregnant. I get Briar's terror in telling her sister now.

"Why are you being so nice to him?" Romy asks.

"Catch you guys later. Let me know when you want to go home," I say on purpose to piss Gillian off, then I go to the guys' table with my beer. I sit beside Danson, and my brothers eye me while they're talking to Jensen and Brooks.

"You're late," Danson says to me.

Bennett and I are the same age, so we've always been close. "Surprised to see you out."

"Grandma and Grandpa for the win," he says and shrugs. "It's been a long time since Wren has spent the night with them, and she's in this stage of wanting to be around women."

"I see that playing out with Briar." I take a pull from my beer.

"Yeah, you're not the only one who loves her. Wren talks about her nonstop." He picks at the label of his beer.

"Love? You're delusional." I sip my beer, my gaze straying over to Briar.

She's listening to Scarlett animatedly talk with her hands. I watch her sip her margarita, and she smiles, looking at it and twirling the straw before taking another sip. She searches me out, and I raise my beer in the air when we make eye contact. The look of appreciation on her face says it all, and if it doesn't prick at my heart a little... fuck.

"Am I really delusional?" My attention turns back to Danson, and he laughs. "Shit, man, you're invested."

I could tell Danson about Briar being pregnant, and he wouldn't tell anyone. He keeps secrets the best out of all my cousins, but it would feel like a betrayal to Briar, so I keep it to myself.

"I think she masturbated to me earlier," I say quietly, still trying to wrap my head around it. I swear, when I knocked, I heard her moan and say my name.

"Are you eavesdropping on the poor woman?"

We both stare toward the dance floor. The live country band is pretty good.

"No, I just heard it when I went to tell her I was ready to go."

"How do you know it wasn't me she was thinking of?" He laughs and takes another pull of his beer, eyeing me over the bottle.

"She said God, and that obviously implies me." I shake my head. "She said my name, but the turnaround is odd since she used to hate me." Then I realize I should ask Danson about her in high school. "Hey, do you remember her from high school?"

"Yeah. She's Gillian's sister, and I remember when Gillian brought her to family stuff, even after Ben left for Clemson."

I scour my memory. "I don't."

"Because you were probably in the barn with whoever was willing."

He's right. In high school, I was a little bit of a man-whore, if I'm honest. I never had a girlfriend and swore against them after I saw what happened to Ben and Gillian when he left for college. Girls liked me, and I took full advantage of it. So during parties at the ranch, I'd always take girls to the barn and make out.

"What do you remember about her?" I ask.

His gaze travels to Briar. "She didn't look how she does now; she's done a one-eighty. I remember her having glasses and braces, and she'd never talk to anyone." He tips his beer in her direction. "She didn't have the confidence she has now. But isn't that the majority of people in high school, with the exception of you?" He twirls the bottle in his hands.

I scour the area for any ears. The other four are at the bar getting refills for everyone now, so I lean in close to Danson. "I have this feeling..."

He laughs but tries to sober up when he sees my face, failing miserably. "Feeling?"

"Yeah, it's weird. I like her living with me. I like having her at my house. I like coming home to her."

His laugh grows louder, garnering the attention of the girls' table.

"Stop laughing. I don't know what to do, and since I heard her coming to imaginings of me—"

"Allegedly," he clarifies.

"I assure you she wasn't thinking of your limp dick." I scowl at him.

"Everyone loves a single dad." He waggles his eyebrows as he sips his beer.

"Whatever. Anyway, what am I supposed to do? Gillian will castrate me." Just the thought of her finding out I touched Briar makes me want to cover my junk.

He pats me on the back. "I know this is a foreign feeling for you, but I say trust it and go with it."

"Go with it?"

He doesn't know the whole story, and I'm sure he'd change his opinion if he knew she's carrying another man's baby. And I know he'd probably be right, but I just can't seem to stop myself from wanting to be involved.

"It's all over your face. Maybe that's why Gillian is so worried. She probably sees it, too."

"What are you talking about? No one sees anything."

He swivels to face me directly, no longer giving me an excuse to look away from him. "You just went behind the bar to make her a drink. She had a place to stay with the girls, but you chose to move her in with you. You're never around anymore except for breakfast. I was down at the barn the other day with Wren to get her on Biscuits, and you weren't there."

My forehead wrinkles. "I was done for the day."

"You used to always work on your reining with Brutus after hours." His eyebrows raise. "I've seen you with her so many times during breakfast, and you're pretty transparent. My mom sees it too."

"You talked to Aunt Darla about it?" *Traitor.*

He chuckles. "No, but I'm gonna give you some advice from a guy who lost his entire world the same day his heart was so full he thought it was going to burst."

"Not the widow shit again."

Danson is always trying to lecture me about time, or lack of it. I feel horrible for what he went through. Just hours after Wren was born, Kristie died. But we're different people.

"You're not guaranteed time." He raises his hand when I try to interrupt. "I'm just saying that if you like her, you'll regret not acting on it. This is the first woman I've ever seen you show any real interest in. Explore it and see what comes of it because if she is the one, you're gonna wish you'd acted sooner. Trust me."

"But—" There's a whole list of reasons why this is a bad idea.

"There will always be reasons not to pursue someone, but if you think this feeling you have is gonna just vanish one day when you wake up, I hate to break it to you, it's not."

I sip my beer, and my gaze falls to Briar's table again.

Damn Danson, I hate when he's right. She is all I think about, all I want. She's something I shouldn't have for more than one reason. The dude ranch, for one. She doesn't need someone like me, someone who has never been in a relationship. Someone who doesn't know how to be in a relationship. What if I fuck it up? This is probably already going to be one of the hardest times of her life. But Danson's right—this need I have for her is something I've never felt for anyone else, and it's only growing by the day.

"As long as you treat her right, I don't think Gillian will be opposed once she sees that you're serious," Danson says.

Gillian turns to me, her eyes narrowing when she sees me looking at Briar.

When did I become the guy who doesn't go after what he wants? It's time I find him again. So I ditch the beer and slide around the table.

"I didn't mean right now," Danson says, but I shake my head.

Standing behind Briar in front of all my cousins, I squat down. "Want to dance?"

Gillian is listening to me, but Laurel is talking about some customers at the bakery.

Briar surprises me and swivels around at the picnic table, sliding her hand in mine. "Sure."

"Um?" Gillian says.

"It's just a dance," I tell her, leading Briar to the dance floor.

"Ben, we're dancing!" Gillian shouts to the guys' table.

I chuckle, pulling Briar into my body and wrapping my one arm around her waist.

I have no idea where this is going, but I do know that this has to go differently than I've ever done things before.

Chapter Twenty-Three

BRIAR

"Why are you doing this?" I ask Emmett, trying to ignore the heat of his hand on the small of my back.

"Because I want to." He twirls me away from Gillian and Ben.

"You're only going to get her mad," I say, my fingers itching to touch the back of his head. To feel the silkiness of the strands between my fingers. I can't imagine what it would feel like to know he was mine, and I could touch him whenever I wanted.

"I'm done caring. I wanted to dance with you, so that's what I'm doing."

He's a good dancer. Of course he is, how could I think any less? Bruce probably gave them lessons in the living room when they were young. He's brought up three great boys.

"But—"

"Just enjoy it." He pulls me closer so that our bodies have hardly any space between them.

In only a few months, I won't be able to get this close to him, so I do what he says and enjoy it. Maybe it's time I take a line from Emmett's book and just live. Do what I want to do. Stop worrying about everyone's reactions to what I decide.

Emmett spins me around, leading me into a slow country song. His fingers dip lower on my back, splaying across the top of my ass.

Every once in a while, Gillian catches my eye. Her eyes fall to his hand, inspecting the closeness of our bodies. Ben looks annoyed, and the two of them fight for who gets to lead because he's trying to get her away, and she wants to stay in line with us. I'm not sure what her problem is or why she's so worried. She's like an overprotective guard dog.

"Ignore her," Emmett whispers. "You're so tense."

"Because she's been eyeing us the whole time."

"If you don't relax, I'm taking you to my truck and driving you home."

I pull back from him, his reaction coming from left field. "Clue me in, Emmett."

He stares down at me, his steps not skipping a beat. "I like you."

"Okay?" I swallow past the dryness in my throat. His facial expression is one I haven't seen yet.

"I mean, I *like* you like you."

My feet stop as my stomach turns over. He tries to get me to dance again, but I don't let him.

"No, you don't." I unwrap my arms from him and walk off the dance floor, panic gripping me.

Instead of sitting at the table with all the girls, I tell them I'm going to the bathroom and walk right out of the bar. I stop in the front parking lot, needing some air.

"Why are you walking away from me?" Emmett asks, busting through the doors.

"Take me home." I wrap my arms around my waist.

"Why? What did I do?" He looks so concerned, so

genuinely worried and confused about what he could've done to upset me.

"Nothing." I shake my head. "I just... I have enough on my plate." My eyes dip to my stomach. We just heard the heartbeat a few days ago. Why is he making everything so confusing?

"And I want to help you."

I blow out a breath and stare at the sky. "Help me? You're not the kind of guy I could ever rely on, Emmett."

I feel like the worst kind of person as soon as the words leave my mouth, but they're true, aren't they?

He steps back, his shoulders falling. His gaze shifts to the door as though he's waiting for someone to come through them. I'm surprised Gillian hasn't stormed out yet. I watch him inhale and exhale a few times.

"Come on." He nods, voice void of emotion. "I'll take you home."

He walks to his truck, not waiting for me. Emmett goes over to the passenger door and opens it before rounding the back of his truck to the driver's side. He climbs in, sits, and waits for me to join him.

What does he expect me to think? That a leopard can change his spots? That I'm the game-changer for him? No one believes in those fairy tales anymore except for maybe Gillian. I'm pregnant with another man's baby. Emmett can't possibly want to start something with me.

Gillian comes out of the door when I'm halfway to the truck. "Are you okay?"

Ben is right behind her.

I stop and turn to face them. "I feel sick. Emmett is going to take me home."

She breaks the distance, and her hands go to my upper arms. I think she still sees me as that six-year-old girl who had nightmares and was afraid of the monsters under her bed. "What is it?"

"Just my stomach. Probably something I ate." I hope I'm putting on an Oscar-worthy performance because I have a feeling when I get in that truck, a bomb is going to explode and upend my life again, shifting everything I was growing comfortable with.

"Okay, well..." Gillian looks at Ben.

He swings his arm over her shoulder. "Call Gill tomorrow. Emmett will get you home safe."

Gillian looks at her soon-to-be husband and smiles at me. "Yeah, he will."

I'm not sure if she believes her words, but I hug her and Ben and walk to the truck.

Emmett's eyes are downcast, focused on the steering wheel as I climb in and buckle my seatbelt. He drives us back to his house, the cab so silent that I feel awkward when I shift in my seat and stare out the window. When he turns the truck down the small road toward his house, I decide I can't go to bed like this. With him mad at me.

He parks, climbs out of the truck, and heads toward the house.

"I'm not sure what you expected. Did you want me to just strip and say, take me?" I'm talking to his back.

He stops on the porch steps, hands sliding into his pockets, but he doesn't turn to face me. "I just wanted to dance with you."

"No." I shake my head and walk toward him. "You told me you *like* me like me. And honestly, that's something a thirteen-year-old boy would say."

He throws his hands in the air and whips around to face me. "So, let me get this straight." He rushes down the steps. "You see me as some playboy who's so stupid I'm willing to jeopardize everything for some pussy."

"What are you talking about?"

He shakes his head. "This isn't something I'd go into lightly. You're not the kind of girl I pick up at The Hidden Cave."

"Exactly. I'm having another man's baby!" I shout. "And spare me the holier-than-thou act. You know your reputation. That reputation was hard-earned by you."

"You're different."

My heart flutters open, allowing his words to warm the part of me that doesn't believe in love anymore, that doesn't think any man can be good and pure in his intentions. "Maybe now, but after you sleep with me and get it out of your system, I'll be like all the rest."

He steps up to me, his hands cradling my cheeks and tipping my head back so he can stare into my eyes. "No, you won't. I understand that it's hard for you to trust right now. Another man just did the worst thing to you, but I'm not him. I can't guarantee you anything except that you are not a fling for me. I would never get involved if it were just about sleeping with you."

I push against his chest. He's saying all the right words, but so did Chad. And I naïvely believed every devotion that came out of his mouth. All to be destroyed when I found out I was probably one of many. That I wasn't his game-changer; I was his Thursday night girl.

"I'm pregnant with another man's baby. I'm spoiled goods." I bolt up the steps, but he grabs my arm, his thumb running along my inner wrist.

"No, you're not."

Tears flood my eyes. "I can't."

He eases me around, and he steps up on the bottom step. "You won't."

I stare at the T-shirt that pulls across his broad shoulders and muscled chest. There are still things he doesn't know. I haven't told him about what I heard, what happened all those years ago.

"I hate you," I whisper.

His hand cradles my neck, thumb running down the front of my throat. He strokes it up and down, tilting my head so I have no choice but to look into his eyes.

"No, you don't." His tone holds so much conviction that my eyebrows scrunch because there's more meaning behind them.

"What?" My forehead wrinkles.

"I'm going to kiss you now, Mrs. Emmett Noughton."

My eyes widen. He leans in, his fingers sliding up the back of my head so I'm exactly where he wants me. How many nights did I stay awake dreaming of this moment? Dreaming of him saying these things to me? But I'm not the only one keeping a secret.

I push him back before our lips meet, and he stumbles down the step, finding his feet. "What the hell?"

"How do you know?"

He laughs.

Anger boils inside me, and I circle around, heading the rest of the way up the porch. "Go to hell!"

I stomp upstairs and slam my bedroom door behind me.

Chapter Twenty-Four

EMMETT

I plop myself on the floor outside Briar's bedroom door. "I'm sorry," I say loudly enough for her to hear me.

I regret trying to be cute, but when she said she hated me, I used the opportunity to let her know I knew that wasn't true. But it didn't go as planned.

"Just go to bed," she says. The hiccup in her voice is killing me.

"I'm not going to go to bed. I want to talk about this."

"I don't."

I rest the back of my head on the door. I want to demand she talk to me. We've been so open with one another to this point, so transparent about all our baggage and our fears. All for it to come down to this...

This is the exact reason I never wanted to get into a relationship with anyone. But with Briar, I'm already in too deep, and I can't find my way out without her holding my hand and guiding me.

"Have you always known?" she asks, her voice closer to me. I think she's on the other side of the door.

"Known what?"

"I'm not stupid, Emmett. You knew what you were doing when you said that." I hear a small thud, and I smile. She is on the other side of the door. She hasn't completely shut me out... yet.

"When I was moving you in, the box with all your keepsakes and yearbooks broke open, and everything fell to the floor."

She groans. "What did you see?"

I huff because, in hindsight, I should've told her that day. Made a joke about it, and we could've moved on. We've come so far since then. I don't want to lose the headway we've made.

"What did I do back then to make you hate me?" This question has been plaguing me.

"Answer me first."

I pull up my legs and rest my forearms on them. "Just scribbles about Mrs. Emmett Noughton. I love Emmett and a big red heart over my senior picture. There were a few other things, but nothing creepy."

"Oh my god." She groans again. "I'm going to bed, and you're going to erase all that from your memory." The floorboards creak.

"I can't blame you, I was hot in high school." I revert to my usual way of making an uncomfortable situation more comfortable.

She chuckles, but it's not the one I've become accustomed to. She's still embarrassed. "Yeah, I was one of your many admirers."

"And I was an idiot." The fact that this beautiful woman pined away for me, and I wasn't aware of it tells me how stupid I was.

"You were a senior and popular. I was a freshman and a geek."

"I'm pretty sure you were the same kind of person you are now. The same one who helped me film and get views. The one who doesn't make me feel like I'm the stupid Noughton brother just because I like to make jokes."

"I shouldn't have said I can't rely on you at the bar."

It sucked hearing those words from her, but the only thing I can do is prove to her—and everybody else—that she's wrong about me. "It's okay. But you're dodging the question."

"Because I don't want to tell you."

"So I did do something." I sigh.

She doesn't say anything, and I worry she might be over this conversation. That she'll open this door with a suitcase in hand and say she's going to Gillian's.

"I'm thankful there's a door between us," she says. "Otherwise, I couldn't gather the nerve."

I wait for her to carry on because in order to make it up to her, I have to know what I did. I can't remember for the life of me.

"The summer after freshman year, Gillian dragged me to your family's annual Fourth of July pig roast. I pretty much sat in a corner the entire time, watching Clayton play with Koa next to me on his game console. I didn't want to be there, but Gillian did, and she deserved a break. Plus, I think it was her first time coming back to your family's home after Ben left. I wanted to support her."

"You're a good sister."

"I can't even tell her I'm pregnant. That I slept with a married man. I'm lying to her every single minute of every day. I'm not a very good sister."

"Let's be honest, she's gone a little psycho lately."

She chuckles. "A little, but I get it. She had no childhood. She was raising Koa and me because my dad had to work all the time. She knows you well and doesn't want me to be hurt. I'm not saying she's right about it, but you have a reputation, Emmett, and I understand her concern."

I nod, although she can't see me. She's right, but I always

thought Gillian saw through my defense mechanisms. That she saw the good that lives inside me. Sure, I preferred one-night stands and flings with no real attachments, but I've never led anyone on. Never lied about my intentions. Does it make me a terrible person that I didn't want a serious relationship until Briar? Until she found a way through my armor?

"So you were at the party," I say to get her back on track.

"You came over, joking with your friends. Said there was a bet that Clayton was Ben's kid. You asked me if you could hold him on your lap, and I said no because you were clearly drunk."

I rack my brain. Senior year, pig roast, me being a jackass as usual. Sounds about right. "My dad let me get drunk?"

"You were eighteen and had graduated by then," she says by way of explanation.

"Kudos for not letting a drunk guy hold a baby. What was Clay? Four?"

"Three. And he did love you. Held his arms out and wanted to go to you. I guess he's always loved you."

"I am the fun Noughton."

A laugh escapes her.

"And then?" I ask.

"And then one of your friends squatted down and looked into Clayton's eyes as if he thought he'd see Ben there."

"Who?"

"James Jackson."

"JJ?"

He left town and never came back after we graduated. I haven't heard anything from or about him since his family no longer lives in the area either. But it makes sense we were betting on Clayton being Ben's. There wasn't much we didn't bet on back then. We were always trying to one-up each other.

"Yeah."

Something in her tone makes my back straighten. Please

tell me JJ didn't do something that means I'm gonna have to search him out and cut off his dick.

"You left, and he stayed," she says.

"But Koa was with you?" My heart rate ramps up, and my body tenses.

"Yeah. But he was giving me a lot of attention. You disappeared for a while."

Of course I did. Fucking idiot. I'm sure I was in the barn.

"He was hitting on me, but I didn't take it seriously. I mean, I knew I wasn't his type. I wasn't a cheerleader, didn't even go to the football games. Well, not without Gillian. It was hard for her to go for a couple of years, but that's another story. But JJ didn't really know who I was, and I wasn't sure why he was giving me attention, but I liked it. I was kind of messed up in the head back then."

"No, you weren't. You were a freshman liking the attention from a senior who a lot of other girls were probably admiring. Did he try something, Briar?"

"No!" The word comes out so fast and adamantly that I believe her. "It's not like that."

"Right, because this circles back to me at some point, right?"

She doesn't say anything for a beat. "Laurel came over and grabbed Clayton, telling me to go enjoy myself, that she'd keep Gillian occupied. Gill was protective, even then. After Laurel left, JJ told me to meet him on the other side of the barn, that he wanted to tell me a secret. Koa wasn't going anywhere, too enthralled in his video game, so I told him I had to use the bathroom."

Dread weighs in my stomach and pins me to the floor as I wait for her to tell me, not remembering one moment of this night. My family has had tons of Fourth of July pig roasts, and I went a little crazy that summer, knowing I was staying in Willowbook. Eating up every minute with my friends, getting drunk, and acting the fool. My dad had a long talk with me that August. That's your summer of fun, he told me, and I should feel privileged because I only got that because I was the youngest.

"Go on." I hold my breath, waiting for her next words.

"I walked to the side of the barn. God, I don't want to tell you..." I hear her groan. "Please can we just move on?"

"I can't make up for it if I don't know what I did."

"You don't have to make up for it. You were young, and I was a nobody."

I frown. "Don't say that. You're not a nobody. Though I have a bad feeling I treated you like that."

Her silence confirms I was a dick.

"Fine. I was walking and heard you and JJ talking so I snuck to the side to eavesdrop. I didn't really want JJ, to be honest. But I felt like if JJ wanted me, maybe you'd notice me. I was so stupid and naïve." She exhales, and all I want to do is hold her. Let her know that was the past, and I'm not that guy, whoever I was, whatever I did.

"You're killing me. Just tell me what I did." I push my hands through my hair.

Her head bangs against the other side of the door. "JJ told you about me meeting him behind the barn, and you asked him why he'd want me. JJ said something I couldn't hear, then a loud girl started trying to pull you away. You told her to go back to the party, and you'd meet her there."

"Carly," I say, a flicker of a memory sparking. "It was Carly Hawkins. She was always loud and clingy."

"Thankfully, she was drunk and didn't notice me, but I was hiding in the shadows of the barn, and there wasn't a lot of light."

"The whole reason it's the make-out spot."

She lets a quiet chuckle loose.

"What did I say?"

"You said I was trash and said everyone would make fun of him if we hooked up because I was a nobody."

The air whooshes from my lungs. When I recover, I ask, "Anything else?"

She grows quiet again, and I know whatever she's going to say is unthinkable for someone her age to have heard. An age when everyone believes what other people think of them.

"That he'd ruin his reputation for a girl who would lie there like a dead fish while he fucked her."

My heart drops to the depths of my stomach like a stone. "Fuck," I say because nothing I can say will change that memory of me.

She doesn't speak.

My mind is spinning. What an asshole my younger self was. How could I ever say that? To speak so vilely of someone? It's not who I've ever been.

"Good night, Briar." I get up from sitting outside her door, walk into my room, and shut the door.

I go into my en suite and turn on the shower, then return to my bedroom and strip off my T-shirt. I need to wash the mental filth covering my skin. I'm a complete and total asshole.

My bedroom door whips open.

"That's it? 'Good night, Briar'?" Her eyes are filled with fire, her hands clenched at her sides.

Chapter Twenty-Five

BRIAR

"What do you want me to say?" Emmett asks, standing shirtless in his bedroom. I hear the shower running in his attached bathroom.

God, he's so damn sexy. I hate the fact that I just relived one of my worst memories, and I'm still drooling over the idiot.

"I don't know, Emmett, maybe 'I'm sorry. I can't believe I was such a dick.' It was really hard to tell you what you said."

He tears his vision away from me, looking at the floor, but I step closer.

"I'm an asshole." His voice is rough like the leather on his cowboy boots.

"Look at me." I get so close I'm almost pressed against him, and I dip my head, not giving him a choice but to meet my gaze.

"What do you want me to say? I'm fucking sorry? Of course I am. Hearing you say that I said those things is tearing me apart, but sorry doesn't take it back. Sorry doesn't rewind time so I can fix it. Sorry doesn't do shit." He steps back and pulls his eyes away from mine.

"I—It would still be a nice thing to say."

"Then I'm sorry." His hands fly up at his sides.

I throw my hands in the air, matching his movement. "Oh, that was heartfelt."

He goes into the bathroom, and I follow him. He's in front of the sink, resting his palms on the counter, back arched and face etched in pain.

"I am so fucking sorry, Briar. I just...I don't know why I would ever be so cruel. The fact that I hurt you like that is killing me. For years you've harbored this hatred for me, and I couldn't figure it out. Why in the hell would you move in with me? Why would you entertain staying here after what I did?"

I sit on the edge of his built-in tub. "I'm not sure I have an answer. But it doesn't matter because you're not that guy, Emmett. My time staying here has taught me that you're not who I thought you were."

He turns around, leaning against the counter and crossing his arms. I'm annoyed with myself that I notice how it makes his biceps and pecs bulge. "I'm not sure about that."

"No—"

He raises his hand. "Don't. Don't sit there and try to make me feel better. I was a son of a bitch, and I'll own it. Don't make excuses for my behavior." He sighs. "I have no idea where we go from here."

My head tips down. I'm not sure how to answer his question. I still can't believe I'm entertaining something with Emmett, and not because of what he did when he was eighteen, but because I'm pregnant... and not with his child.

"I don't know. I'm having a baby. You're the only one who knows. I'm scared, Emmett." My tears break free. Tonight has been way too emotional, and these damn hormones make it impossible to push down my feelings.

"I'm scared, too, but I've never felt like this. Ever."

I laugh at how bizarre this moment is. "How can we even

entertain this? I'm going to be huge in a couple of months. I'm not going to be this version of myself ever again. I won't ever have the freedom to come and go as I please again. My body will never look like this again."

"Is that what you think? That it's your body I want?" He pushes off the counter and sits next to me.

"I think that's part of it. And to be honest, I'm afraid it might be a little of you wanting what you can't have. But nothing will change the fact that this baby isn't yours. That we're going to try to have a relationship when I haven't even told the biological father about the baby."

He buries his head in his hands, running them up and down his face and groaning. "First of all, you're hot as hell, and that's not going to change either when you show or after. So yes, I am attracted to you, but I've been attracted to a lot of women in my life."

"Gee, thanks," I deadpan.

He turns and looks at me, and I don't even get a smirk. *Okay then.*

"I don't just want you because you're gorgeous, Briar. It's because you're you. It's the way you come back at me with jokes and give as good as you get. It's you making me dinner because I let you stay here. It's you taking my idea seriously and helping to try to make it successful. It's you, plain and simple. You just happen to come in a really smokin' hot package." I finally get his flirtatious smirk, and the light in his eyes returns.

"You're making this hard."

"What's hard? Other than me once I get you in that shower."

His humor undoes me, and all that runs through my mind is my earlier masturbation session.

"I'm not sure I'm ready for that."

"Fair enough." He slides closer, his hand moving over my leg and falling into mine. "I'll wait."

We sit there, side by side, holding hands like teenagers. The fact is that there are a plethora of reasons this shouldn't work between us. But the comfort I feel when I'm with him is something I've never felt with anyone, not even Chad, who I thought I loved. These feelings I have for Emmett are so hard for me to place, let alone dissect. At the same time, I can't help but wonder what it would feel like for him to hold me.

"I forgive you," I whisper.

He doesn't say anything, and I look at him, wanting him to know that I do forgive him for what happened all those years ago. He's not that same person.

"Nope. Not yet."

"What?" I shake my head, forehead wrinkled.

He turns his head, locking eyes with me. "Not until I prove to you that I'm not that guy."

"You don't have to prove anything." I squeeze his hand.

He falls to his knees and shuffles in front of me, then places his hands on my hips. I open my thighs, allowing him in. "I do. I need to prove to you that I'm not that guy. That I'm not who everyone else thinks I am. That you're my game-changer. My anomaly. My person."

"Emmett." My hands go to his at my sides, about to drag them off me because he doesn't need to say these things for us to move forward. He can't possibly mean them.

"I told you to let me prove it. So when you're ready, you let me know." He draws back, takes my wrist, and places a kiss on the inside.

He releases my hand, but I grip his, and his eyes question what I'm doing.

"I'm ready," I say in a rush.

He shakes his head and rises to his feet. "No, you're not, and it's okay. I'm a patient man."

He walks toward his shower, and I stand, steeling myself.

Take what you want, Briar.

"You stupid man," I say.

He circles back around and tilts his head. "I thought we already clarified that."

I step toward him. "You're not going to tell me when I'm ready and when I'm not."

His lips tip up at the corners, but he's fighting it.

I step forward again. "Whether you meant to or not, you've shown me how I should be treated." Another step closer. "As if I'm a prize." One more step. "You've stood by my side, supported me, haven't pushed me. I never saw you coming, Emmett. You bulldozed into my life at the worst possible time, flipping it on its axis. As scared as I am, I'm going to trust that you'll catch me if I fall."

"I will." His eyes are so earnest as they look into mine.

I approach his chest, rise to my tiptoes, and wrap my arms around his neck. "Kiss me."

His arm swings around me, pulling me into his hard chest, and he bends his neck. "I thought you'd never ask."

I giggle, but his lips fall to mine, swallowing my laugh. His lips are firm, and his five-o'clock shadow burns my face in the most delicious way.

The need to explore him with my hands burns in my veins. To feel that hard body I've been admiring for weeks. But I'm lost in the needy sounds coming from his throat as his mouth crushes mine.

All that desire that's pooled over my time here intensifies into a deep ache between my legs. I feel as if I'm lost in another dimension. His kiss is soul-crushing, and in that moment, I know he's ruining me. If this doesn't work out with us, I'll never kiss another man again without thinking of Emmett.

Finally, my hands push into the silkiness of his hair, running up and down the back of his head, not wanting him to wake me from this dream state. He hauls me up, and my legs wrap around his waist so that I feel the hardening of his bulge in his jeans. He's no longer gentle, his tongue thrusting into my mouth. I meet him stroke for stroke, unable to get close enough to him.

He carries me through the doorway into his bedroom but doesn't lay me down on his bed. And I'm not complaining—I'd glue myself to him if he continues the slow strokes of his tongue, his bulging biceps holding me up. My nipples pebble, my breasts heavy with need.

His lips pull away from mine, leaving them swollen and stinging. "Is this okay? What about the baby?"

His breathing is labored, and the little freshman girl inside me cheers that I did that to him. I'm the one taking my crush to the brink of want.

He lowers me to the mattress, but I don't release his neck, so his lips fall to my neck.

"It's fine. The baby will be fine," I assure him and loosen my hold to allow his exploration of my neck and collarbone. "I thought you were showering?" I'm more than happy to join him.

"Later. Don't rush this."

"No rushing," I practically pant.

His hands slide up the hem of my shirt, pushing it over my head. "That day in the white dress... just so you know, we're reenacting that without a bra or panties."

He reaches behind me and unhooks my bra. I help him take it off, and his gaze fixes on my nipples.

"I knew you'd have perfect nipples." He bends, taking one in his mouth.

I suspected Emmett would be a talker, but he's ratcheting up this orgasm one step higher with every desire he's confessing. I arch my back, my hands going to my jeans, unbuttoning and lowering the zipper.

He strips his mouth off me and stares at me. "That's my job."

"Then get me naked."

That million-dollar smile hits me full force, and I inch up, capturing his lips in a fevered kiss, never getting enough of him. His fingers hook in my jeans, and I lift my hips to get them off. He takes my jeans and underwear in one go, leaving me completely bare beneath him.

He stands in front of my open legs, and his fingers manipulate the button of his jeans. His muscled chest and the intensity in his eyes staring down at me remind me of a caged animal who can only be patient with its prey for so long. He quickly unzips his jeans, pushing them down with his boxer briefs. His dick springs free, and lord, is it everything I thought it'd be.

"Now I'm a little worried about the baby."

He laughs, and his head falls back. "I love that fucking mouth of yours."

"Wait until you see what else it can do."

His dick twitches at my words, and he slides his hand down his length, pumping it a few times, his gaze soaking up every inch of my body as though he's committing it to memory. I melt into the softness of his mattress, eager for what's next.

"I've been recently tested. I don't have any STIs," he says.

"Same. And clearly, you can't get me pregnant twice."

His nostrils flare, and his Adam's apple bobs. "Are you telling me what I think you are?"

He's still stroking himself, and I'm mesmerized by the vision. I nod.

"I can take you bare?" he clarifies, and I laugh.

"Well, if you'd rather use a condom."

He bends one knee on the bed, the mattress dipping, then hovers over me, his weight about to bear down on me. "Not a chance." He shakes his head, swiping a finger along my folds until his eyes flutter closed. "So wet and ready."

"I've been ready for a long time."

Our gazes meet and hold, and he positions the tip at my opening. Inch by inch, he slides inside me, placing his lips on mine and kissing me until he stretches me in the most glorious way when he's fully seated inside me.

His lips leave mine, and he grunts. "Shit, you're about to make me a two-minute man."

I bring his mouth back to mine, lost in this private space we've created for each other.

He circles his hips and draws in and out of me, and I grow wetter with every stroke. His tongue licks up my neck, then he nibbles my earlobe. Hearing and feeling his breath intensifies every sensation.

"Harder," I say.

"I don't want to—"

"Harder," I repeat.

He listens, drilling in and out of me. My hands fall to the comforter, gripping it while my hips rise off the bed, meeting him thrust for thrust. It's all too much. This. All the tension we've been living with. The electrifying small touches. The discreet glimpses at each other.

My moans turn into cries, and everything in the room blurs until all I can feel, see, and hear is Emmett. Only Emmett. Only *us*.

His eyes lock with mine, so transparent. All the promises he wants to deliver on, everything he wants me to see in him, it's all alive inside of them.

I bring his mouth to mine again and come so hard I buck and clench around his dick. He grunts and groans, not moving until I can't hold the kiss anymore from the euphoric feeling inside me.

"Next time, I'm watching," he says, getting up on his

elbows and grinding in and out of me at the same pace he was. His one hand squeezes my breast, showing me how strong he is. "God, Briar, you're killin' me."

He mumbles a curse before he pumps inside me, stilling with a loud groan, then lowers his body to mine.

He pushes my blonde hair off my forehead and kisses me again. "Are you okay?"

"I'm great," I say, running my hands through his sweaty hair.

"Thank you."

"For what?"

"For trusting me."

It's the expression in his eyes that makes my nose tickle as wetness pools in my eyes. There's so much conviction in them and gratitude that someone is taking a chance after seeing the real him. And I feel so privileged to be the one chosen.

Chapter Twenty-Six

EMMETT

Am I having an out-of-body experience? How the hell did I get here? Not that I'm complaining. Having Briar lying on me with my fingers lazily going up and down her arm isn't something I ever thought I wanted. Until her. Until she flipped my life upside down.

"I really am sorry about what I said." God, I can't conceive of why I'd ever have said that shit about her.

Briar turns to me, resting her chin on my chest. "I already told you I forgive you. Let's forget it, okay?"

I swallow past the dryness in my throat. I don't know that I'll ever be able to stop thinking about how I said something so mean about someone. My dad raised me better.

She places her hand on my cheek. "I'm serious, Emmett, stop thinking about it."

I nod, but it's not going to stop infiltrating my mind.

"I feel like I just stacked on another problem," Briar says. "Gillian isn't going to be happy with either one of us."

I don't say anything at first because I'm unsure how to word what I want to convey. "I know your life is really complicated right now and that you have a lot of decisions to make involving you and the baby." Her eyes soften and the smallest smile creases her lips, so I say, "But I want to be part of the equation."

"What do you mean?"

I sit up in bed, and she sits up on her knees, the sheet slipping off her body. I force my gaze to stay trained on her eyes so she knows how serious I am about this.

"I just want to fit into the life you choose, but I know I might not." My chest tightens, waiting for her to respond.

"Did you forget what we just talked about?" She climbs onto my lap, straddling me, and places her hands on my cheeks. "You're in the equation, Emmett. I didn't sleep with you to get you out of my system. I slept with you because I want this. Wherever it's going, I want it."

"But—"

She shakes her head. "No but. Stop feeling guilty for the stupid shit you said in high school and stop doubting this."

I slide my hand over her belly, holding it there. "I just want you to have the best life."

She kisses me. "Then that includes you. You fit... always."

I nod, and my teeth press into my bottom lip.

"Say I believe you, Briar."

"I believe you, Briar," I repeat, humor in my voice.

"And thank you."

My forehead wrinkles. "For?"

"Telling me what you want so I don't have to question you later or read into things. I really like transparency. It probably comes from having a loving mother one day, and then she's gone the next. Always be truthful with me. That's all I ask."

I roll her onto her back and position my body over hers. "I like this side of you. Telling me what you want."

"I'm taking a lesson out of Wren's book."

"Good girl." I kiss her stomach.

Her hands fall over my head, her nails scraping my scalp, which I love. "Do I get a reward now? A gold star sticker?"

I look up at her, my lips casting small kisses along her stomach. "You're about to get more than a gold star."

I get up on my knees, bringing her right leg up to my mouth. I trail kisses along her strong calf, my gaze fixed on hers with every nibble or lick. Her chest rises and falls, her breaths becoming more labored the closer I get to her core. I graze my fingers along her inner thigh, barely touching the apex of her thighs.

"You're torturing me," she says, reaching for her tits.

Her hips rise off the mattress as if that's going to make me give her what she wants. She grunts in frustration when I lower my stomach to the mattress, widening her legs with both hands and blowing a stream of hot air onto her pussy.

"Emmett..."

I chuckle, peeking my head up. "Yeah, sweetheart?" I swipe my tongue over her, and she groans, rising on her elbows to watch me. "Better?"

She stares at me with that death glare I know she means to be intimidating, but sometimes it's just hot as fuck.

"Not yet," she says.

"Let me try again." With the tip of my tongue, I flick her clit several times.

She cries out, her fingers twisting her nipples.

"How about now?"

"You know what I want." She tries to raise her pussy to my lips, but we're not gonna play that game. I'm going to enjoy the hell out of getting her right to the edge before I devour her.

"You taste as sweet as I thought you would." I lower my head and suck on her clit, twirling my tongue around it. I let it pop out of my mouth, and she grunts.

"I swear to god, Emmett."

"You swear what?"

"You're never getting a blow job if you keep this up." Her voice is menacing, and I laugh. "You know what? I don't need you." She tries to turn to the right.

I stop her with my hands on her thighs. She falls to her back, and I open her legs as wide as they'll go, which is pretty fucking wide. How blessed am I to fall for a yoga instructor?

Without playing any more games, I worship her.

Her back falls to the mattress, and her hands fist the comforter. "Finally."

I run my hands over and up her outer thighs, grabbing her ass and bringing her pussy to my mouth. She grinds along my tongue, desperate for the friction, but this is my ship to navigate. My hands run up her stomach, and I take over cupping her breasts and tweaking her nipples.

Her back arches and her cries grow louder and louder. Watching her increases my pace. I want to get her to the edge and see her free fall over. To know that I did that to her. My mouth, my tongue, my hands took her there.

She shouts my name. "Oh god." She comes so hard, she practically tries to suffocate me with her thighs.

I take one long lick of her before climbing up her body, stopping at one of her tits to suck it into my mouth.

"Best ever, right?" I say to her when I reach her mouth.

"Yeah," she whispers. "I've never come that hard from that."

"Don't worry, sweetheart, I'll lick your pussy all day, every day if you want."

She slaps my shoulder, and I laugh, falling to my back and pulling her down with me.

The sun is just starting to make its presence known. We'll have Sunday dinner tonight, but we have hours and hours before that.

Her stomach growls.

"You and the baby need food." I slide out from under her. "I'll be right back."

Her arm anchors to my side, and she locks it so I can't move. "Not yet."

I get what she means, wanting to preserve this moment, so I relax back in bed. Outside this room is the real world. The real world where so many questions need answers. The real world where people might not believe us when we tell them how much we care for each other.

"Can we keep this between us for a little bit?" Her voice is small and unsure.

I blow out a breath because I want everyone to know she's mine. But I understand how difficult this is, given her situation.

I kiss her forehead and wrap my arms around her. "Sure, I'll be your dirty little secret."

"It's not like that." She pulls back, looking straight into my eyes.

I nod. "I know. I know."

She kisses my chest, and her fingers circle along my abs. And we allow ourselves to live in this bubble we've created for ourselves a little longer.

Chapter Twenty-Seven

BRIAR

Emmett parks his truck far away from the field.

"So, can I cheer for you?" I cringe because it's a dumb question, but I don't want anyone to see through us.

"Hell yes." He grabs my hand and tugs me to his side in the cab. "I can't wait until I can put the Emmett's girl shirt on you and kiss you before a game."

My heart warms with a soft, comforting glow. I want that too.

"I know I have to tell Gillian," I say, but what we have is so nice without anyone knowing.

This week, we both came home at the end of the day, showered, and fell into bed with one another. Emmett's taken me in the kitchen while I was making dinner, on the couch while I watched my favorite show, and in the middle of the night. His house has turned into a love nest, our love nest, and I don't want to bring in anyone who's going to point their finger and tell us it will never work. I love Gillian, but she'd be the first one to do that.

"Yeah, you do," he says.

Emmett hasn't pushed me to tell people, but I can feel his

impatience growing. It makes me happy that he wants to tell everyone we're a couple.

"I want it too, so you know. I want to go to those bleachers and give you a good luck kiss. Maybe have you squeeze my ass."

He smiles.

"And I want to jump and cheer when you score, letting all those women know you're mine."

He wraps his arm around my shoulders and runs his hand down my hair. "I know you do."

I kiss the hollow of his neck. "Thanks for being understanding."

He kisses the top of my head. "I better get you out of here before anyone comes along."

I put my hand on his cheek, turning his head to face me and crush my lips to his. I slide my tongue into his mouth, and he grabs my waist, tugging me onto his lap. Our kiss grows in intensity.

Before we pass the point of no return, I lean back. "Good luck tonight."

His hands run down my sides, and he squeezes my ass with both hands. "Try not to ogle me too hard."

"That's a hard ask." I've been ogling him since I came to my first game last year when I visited. It's nice knowing I'm going to go home with him this time.

He pats my ass. "Time to go."

I slide off his lap and climb out of the truck from the passenger side. He gets out and shuts his door, rounding the back of his cab to grab his bag and looking to make sure no one saw us. His hand moves to grab my hand, but I slide it away, clasping my hands in front of me. He groans and dips his head back toward the sky but doesn't say anything.

We walk up to the bleachers, Emmett's finger grazing my ass before anyone notices, and he heads to the dugout.

"Hey, you," Gillian says, patting the spot next to her on the bleachers. "I saved you a spot."

I climb the bleacher, seeing her shirt that says, Ben's girl. Sadie is sporting her Jude's girl shirt stretched out over her swollen belly, and I silently bemoan not being able to wear a shirt for Emmett.

"Briar!" Wren rushes out of the dugout.

"Wren!" Bennett shouts after her. "You're the mascot."

Wren waves him off. "I don't wanna be anymore."

Bennett rolls his eyes, and all the women in the stands laugh.

Wren climbs the bleachers, sliding between Gillian and me. Why thank you, Wren.

"Daddy let me come tonight." She wiggles in her seat, her hand going to my hair. "I like your waves."

"Thank you," I say and touch her braid. "Who did your hair?"

"Romy did it in the dugout. She said she doesn't want to play today."

"No worries, I made it!" Brooks comes out of nowhere and raises his hands. He's still wearing his sheriff's vest over his Plain Daisy Ranch shirt and baseball pants.

He rounds the edge of the dugout and disappears inside.

"Seriously, Brooks, everyone knows you're the sheriff. You can take the vest off," I hear Lottie say.

"So, how are things?" Gillian asks, ignoring the commotion in the dugout.

"Good. Just been working." Thankfully, I haven't started showing that much, but it'll be impossible to hide soon, especially because summer is coming, which means I can't hide my belly with sweaters.

"'Cause you said you didn't feel good last weekend, and I keep missing you on the phone."

Which is because I always time my calls so I can leave a

voicemail. She must be busy because she hasn't popped in on a surprise visit.

I shrug. "I've tried to reach you a couple times."

She nods. "And living with Emmett? How's that going?"

"Great. He's easy to live with."

Gillian nods again. "You know he's not talking to his brothers, right?"

"He said something about that. Have they not resolved it yet?"

"No. He lets Jude tell him what needs to be done on the ranch, but that's about it from what I hear."

Wren puts her hand in mine, and I silently thank her for saving me from the interrogation that Gillian's just ramping up.

"Do you think they're going to win?" Wren asks.

I look at her small hand in my larger one, and the fact that someday soon, that will be my son or daughter's hand hits me. I have to take a deep breath before I can answer.

"I'm sure. Don't they always win?" I didn't see a lot of last season, but I thought they were doing well.

"No, Wild Bull Ranch won." Walker Matthews walks up holding what I assume is the league trophy.

"He won." Wren thumbs in his direction with an annoyed look on her face.

He is annoying. Tried to hit on me last year.

"Why are you here, Walker?" Sadie asks.

"To scout out this year's competition. It's the first game of the season after all." He sits on the bleacher in front of us.

"We're playing Diamond Spur Ranch, and they're made up of five brothers plus crew," Gillian tells me. "They're pretty good when they all get along, which is rare."

"I heard they have some new stud this year. That's why I'm here," Walker says.

Sadie rolls her eyes and sighs.

He looks up at us, and his eyes fix on me. "Look who's back this year."

Wren's hand clasps mine harder. "She's Emmett's!" She narrows her small eyes at him.

"What?" Gillian's head whips in my direction.

"Wren, I'm just his roommate." I give her a smile.

She shakes her head. Did Emmett tell Bennett, and he let it slip to his daughter?

"Yes, Wren. They're just sharing space for the moment," Gillian says.

Walker chuckles. "We all know Emmett doesn't see anyone exclusively. He usually picks them up after I'm done with them."

Gillian's hands go over Wren's ears. "What is wrong with you? There's a little girl around. You shouldn't even be here."

Walker cringes, looking somewhat repentant. "Sorry, she's usually not at the games."

"I'm six now, so Daddy said I can come." She wiggles her shoulders, giving him attitude. It's kind of cute. "Watch what you say."

Wren looks at me, and I nod in agreement that she told him off. She puts one foot up on the bleacher in front of her, crossing her leg over it. She's so cute.

The umpire calls the coaches in, and Jude goes to home plate along with the coach of the Diamond Spurs. They do what they do, and a coin is flipped.

"We're home," Jude says, and all the players go to their positions on the field.

Emmett eyes me from shortstop, then his attention falls on Walker.

"There's Daddy!" Wren points toward left field. Bennett waves, and she claps for him. "And Emmett. Do you see him?"

Gillian is staring from Wren to me.

"I do. Shortstop."

Wren snuggles closer to me, and again, Gillian's eyes shift to our clasped hands.

The first player goes up to bat. Scarlett pitches and the ball goes right between third and shortstop. Emmett and Ben race for the ball. Emmett says he's got it, but Ben continues for it, so Emmett bulldozes him with his shoulder.

"Whoa," Gillian says. "That was unnecessary."

Ben falls to the ground and Emmett gets the ball, throwing it to first. They get the runner out. Ben gets up, brushing dirt off his legs, and Emmett says something I can't hear.

I don't say anything to Gillian.

The next batter strikes out, and the one after that hits a fly ball. Wren stands, watching her dad run for the ball, but Lottie comes in to catch it from centerfield.

"That was a good catch," Wren says as if she's convincing herself.

"It was."

Then we're up to bat.

"Looks like he changed the lineup this year," Gillian says to Sadie.

"You don't want to know how much he's stressed about this." Sadie shakes her head.

Ben comes out of the dugout first. He used to be the four-hitter if I remember correctly. He looks pissed off, but goes up to bat, swings at the first pitch, and gets a line drive to right field, safe at first.

The second batter is Lottie, who also gets on by an error from the third baseman.

Brooks comes out of the dugout. "Maybe if you weren't staring at her ass, you wouldn't have bobbled the ball," he calls to the third baseman before going back in to sit down.

"So protective," Walker says. "What's going on with them?"

"Nothing," everyone says in unison, though I think we all believe something is happening there.

With two runners on base, Romy is next up to bat. She drags her bat and rolls her eyes. "Why would you put me third? Last year I had a negative average."

"What's up with her?" Sadie asks Gillian.

Gillian shakes her head. "I don't know. She's never liked playing, but she's usually more into it."

Wren's mouth crinkles as though she doesn't know either.

Romy bunts and runs to first. The catcher and pitcher don't know whose ball it is, so she's safe. Wren jumps up and down, clapping.

Then Emmett comes out of the dugout, and the way Wren screams his name, you'd think he's a celebrity. She turns to me. "Emmett's up!"

I can't help but chuckle at her enthusiasm. "I see."

"Am I missing something?" Gillian asks, eyes narrowed.

I shake my head.

Emmett gets into position, and I admire his physique and feel proud that he's mine. No one here knows it, but this man has been giving me record-worthy orgasms for the past week.

The first pitch is a strike.

"He can't handle the fourth spot. He's too explosive," Walker chimes in with his opinion.

"Shut up, you bully," Wren says.

If I was her mom, I might discipline her or tell her to sit down on the bench, but I'm not, and she's right. Walker Matthews needs to keep his mouth shut.

The next pitch comes in, and Emmett swings and misses. I bite my lip, worried that maybe I'm bad luck. I saw him strike out so many times last year.

Another pitch comes in, and he swings, connecting the bat to the ball, and it sails over the infield, dropping right between second base and centerfield. Ben hustles to score, and Lottie gets to third while Emmett is at first.

Unfortunately, not much happens after that. The next inning, Emmett and Ben are back in the infield. A pop up comes their way that Emmett is camped under, but Ben shoves him out of the way, catching the ball.

Emmett gets up and storms at Ben, tackling him and shouting, "What the fuck?"

I place my hands over Wren's ears.

They battle for dominance, rolling around as if they're nine years old. Ben gets a punch in on Emmett, then Emmett nails Ben across the cheek with his fist.

"Brother brawl," Walker says.

I want to kick him off the bleachers.

All the rest of the Plain Daisy Ranch players go over, and Jude gets in the middle of them. Emmett and Ben eventually get to their feet, both holding their cheeks.

"He's only letting you bat fourth to make you happy because you act like a fucking baby," Ben shouts.

Emmett goes after Ben again, but Jude gets in the mix, holding him back. But then Ben yells at Jude, and pretty soon, it's a three-way fight, all the brothers shouting at each other.

Sadie grabs my hand. "They'll work it out. They always do."

I'm not sure what the look on my face must be that would make her tell me that.

"Everything will be all right," she says, squeezing my hand.

I turn to her, and she smiles sweetly, as Sadie always does.

Fear pricks my spine. Does she know?

"If they could only control their tempers," Gillian says.

Wren goes to the fence line. "Stop beating up Emmett!"

Bennett comes over to the fence and bends down to talk to her.

"I wish I had this on video," Walker says. "Left my phone in the truck though."

Gillian puts her foot on his back, pushing him off the bleachers. He stumbles and turns toward her.

"Sorry, I was stretching and didn't realize you were so close." She shrugs with a saccharine smile.

In a huff, Walker takes his trophy and leaves.

All three brothers continue to yell and point fingers while the rest of the cousins hover around the backstop, waiting for them to finish.

Chapter Twenty-Eight

EMMETT

Ben's tires skid as he hauls ass out of the parking lot.

Jude drives away too.

I'm left on the bleachers with Briar, Wren, and Bennett, holding an ice pack that the Diamond Spurs gave me because my asshole brothers wouldn't share the first aid kit with me.

"What's going on with you guys?" Bennett asks, watching Wren drag a stick through the dirt at the bottom of the bleachers.

"We're fighting." My head is rocking.

Briar's keeping her distance, not wanting to give away that we're a couple, although Bennett pretty much assumes we are from our conversation at The Hidden Cave. Though I never officially confirmed it.

"You're always fighting about something. Want to talk about it?"

"Not really." I lean my head down, my eye swelling. "The worst part is Ben taught me how to punch, and I still can't beat him."

"I don't know, his face looked just as bad," Briar says.

"I hate you." Wren hops from one foot to the other like a boxer in the ring preparing to fight. "No, I hate you. Pow, pow, pow!" She pretends to throw punches.

"Great, I've turned her into Mike Tyson." The memory of that night at the pig roast that Briar told me about is still itching away at me. "Hey, Danson, was I an asshole in high school?"

He laughs. "You were cocky."

Briar smiles and nods.

"That's what the girls loved about me." I play the part everyone wants me to. Always have. "But was I mean to people? Like, did I talk shit and stuff?"

Danson knew me the best out of anyone. Jude was working the ranch. Ben was busy with football my first two years, then he was off at college. Bennett was like my twin brother. We were inseparable.

"Why do I feel like you're asking me this for a specific reason?" Bennett frowns.

I glance at Briar.

"I told you I forgive you," she says.

"I know, but I'm still sulking about it and wondering why I did it."

"Did what?" Bennett looks between us.

He definitely knows we're a couple, I can tell by his expression, but he'll wait until we're alone to ask me. He'd never put Briar on the spot, and he knows Ben and Gillian's stance on us.

"Fourth of July pig roast the year we graduated."

"Okay..." He glances Wren's way to make sure she hasn't wandered off, then he looks back at me.

"JJ was there," I say.

"The two of you got into a fight." He nods as if I remember it.

"We did?"

"Yeah." He looks at the sky. "I think it was about Carly, maybe. You were back behind the barn with her, and then you and JJ came out shouting at one another. I went over to break it up before you got close to the party and the adults noticed."

I look at Briar again, and she stiffens.

"No, wait. Carly was there, but... oh yeah." His eyes go to Briar and widen. "It was about you."

"Are you sure?" What the hell could we have fought over about Briar? I barely knew her then.

"Yeah, I think JJ was trying to get with you." He looks at Briar again. She shows no sign of knowing what he's talking about, and that seems to confuse him even more. "You told him not to, and he came at you, saying you were jealous, probably wanted her for yourself and to stay out of his business. He left the party not long after that. Carly went off somewhere, and when I asked you what happened, you said Ben would kill you if you let something happen to Briar."

She gasps.

"Wait... what?" My head tilts, and I cringe when it aggravates my swollen face.

"I'm sorry, Briar, ahead of time for saying this." He looks at Wren. "Hey, kiddo, do you see that rock over there? Can you get it? We'll paint it tomorrow."

She nods and runs in the direction he pointed while Briar and I wait for him to fill us in.

"You said JJ was bragging about how he was gonna take her virginity, and you tried reverse psychology or something to get him off her scent. He said she wasn't worth his time or something to that effect. I can't remember exactly."

Relief floods my veins. I still regret that she overheard me and has been carrying that with her ever since, but knowing I did it to protect her helps to ease some of my guilty conscience.

Wren runs back with the rock in her hand, all smiles.

Bennett looks apologetically at Briar, but damn, I'm thankful for his memory.

"Daddy, I'm hungry," Wren says, handing the rock to him. "Want to come over and paint rocks tomorrow?" she asks Briar and me.

"Maybe. We'll see," I tell her.

"I gotta go, keep ice on it. Take care of him, Briar." He chuckles.

They walk away, Bennett holding Wren's hand.

"I don't like Ben, he hit Emmett," I hear her say.

He says something to her, but I can't make it out.

"Why did you ask him? I told you I forgave you." Briar sits right next to me since we're the last ones here.

"I don't know. He still remembers algebra from high school. I knew he would've been there that night, and if something big went down, I would've told him about it. It's been killing me that I hurt you, and I wanted to see what he knew about what the hell I was thinking."

"Well, I'm glad we found out the truth. Now you can rest easy knowing you were trying to protect me, not hurt me." She takes my hand. "I wasn't going to let him sleep with me."

"No surprise that I didn't trust JJ. Ben would've wanted me to watch out for you even if he and Gillian weren't together at the time."

"It doesn't matter. It's in the past, but thank you."

I turn to her and run my palm over her cheek. "It mattered to me. I didn't want to be that guy. Ever. Even as a punk-ass high schooler. I want to be a good guy, a guy you're proud to call yours."

She smiles and kisses my cheek. "I am."

"Good, now thank me for being your Prince Charming."

She pushes my shoulder, swipes my truck keys off the top of my bag, and walks away.

"Hey," I say, following her.

I probably look like a love-sick puppy chasing its owner, but I am. Happily.

Chapter Twenty-Nine

EMMETT

This morning, I left a note on Briar's yogurt in the fridge that said tonight is date night and to be ready at seven. It's hard to have a date night when we can't go out in public around here, but I have a good friend in Hickory who owns a drive-in. I got him to agree to open it for the night for us only. He's playing some older romance movie, but I don't really care what's on the screen if I get to spend time with Briar.

I walk into my house at six thirty, and I hear her getting ready upstairs. I love coming home to her. I never thought I'd be the guy who couldn't get home fast enough at the end of the day, but here I am, head over heels for this woman.

I climb the stairs and right away notice she's getting ready in her room. It feels odd since she's been spending most of her time in my room, even doing her makeup and hair in my bathroom lately. I knock on her bedroom door.

"You'll see me at seven," she says.

I chuckle and head into my room, seeing a new pair of jeans and a plaid shirt with the metal snaps as buttons laid out on the bed with a note that says wear me. I grin.

"Reversing roles, I see," I call, and she giggles. I'll never tire of that sound.

I take a shower, do my hair, dress in the outfit she picked out, and spray on some cologne. I already set everything up to make it a surprise.

At seven o'clock, I knock on her door again.

She opens it, and my breath halts. "Fuck, you're gorgeous."

Her dress is white and lacy, and her hair is done in waves. Her makeup is heavier than usual, which she doesn't need, but it highlights her beautiful eyes.

"I can't believe you're my date tonight."

She laughs, grabbing her purse from the bed before coming back over to me. She lifts onto the balls of her feet and kisses me, and although I want to keep her pressed to my mouth, we have to get to the movie.

I put out my hand for her to go down the stairs first. My eyes stay trained on her, still disbelieving that this woman picked me.

We go to my truck, and I open the passenger door for her. She climbs up and puts on her seat belt.

I go to the driver's seat, and before I turn on the engine, I lean over for another kiss. "I'm the luckiest guy ever."

She shakes her head. "Stop. I'm blushing."

"And I love seeing it on your skin."

"Just go."

She looks embarrassed, and I'm not sure why. Surely she knows the catch she is. Obviously, the men before me didn't make her feel like the prize she is, but I'm determined to change that.

We drive toward Hickory, and she doesn't ask any questions. She doesn't even ask for a hint about where we're going.

I glance at her. "You like surprises, huh?"

"Love them," she says.

I wish I could watch her the entire drive, but I keep my eyes on the road, reaching for her hand. She accepts my advance and squeezes my hand.

I can't explain this thing between us or how I fell for her. I've always been the guy who swore off relationships, but Briar has changed everything, which I still find crazy.

I pull into the deserted drive-in, and for the first time tonight, she looks confused. "Um..."

"Don't worry. I've got it handled."

I'm not sure if she was questioning the fact that it's not open or that it's still so cool at night, how could we watch it in comfort, but I've got it covered, and I don't want her to worry.

"Okay." She relaxes back in her seat.

I drive the truck to the middle of the gravel lot. A blown-up inflatable couch sits on a giant blanket with pillows, sleeping bags, and blankets. I bought almost every kind of candy at the store because I didn't know her favorite, along with popcorn and chips.

"Emmett," she says, sitting up straighter to take in the scene.

I park the truck to the side of my setup, so it can block the breeze a little, and shift to look at her. "Surprise."

She opens her door and gets out before I can stop her and tell her that's my job from now on. Immediately she slips off her shoes, sits on the couch, and fingers through the candy. "This is amazing."

I take off my cowboy boots and walk over to her. "I know it's not a five-star hotel or the opera. You're accustomed to more high-end things in Chicago, I'm sure."

She stands and places her finger over my lips. "It's perfect. So perfect."

I take her in my arms because it's hard not to have her close to me every second of every day. We don't kiss, but she rests her head on my chest, allowing me to hold her.

I never want us to end, but I can't deny that I fear what the future holds. There are so many unknowns, and her waiting to tell Gillian about the baby, about us, is really wearing on me. I want everyone to know she's mine. Maybe then they'll see that I'm not the person they thought I was. That she's changed me. But even if they don't, it doesn't matter as long as she knows.

There's also the matter of wanting to bring her to my mom's grave to introduce Briar to her. I need to thank Mom for sending Briar to me, because I know she had something to do with it.

"I didn't know your favorite candy, so I bought one of everything." We both sit down on the couch.

"I noticed you have quite the selection." She pulls out a pack of Reese's Pieces. "My favorite."

"Noted." I lean back on the couch, my arm swung over the back, watching her open the package and eat the first one.

Briar grabs a blanket, slides against my side, and covers both of us with it. Then she stares up at me, and I kiss her on her temple.

"This is the most thoughtful thing anyone has ever done for me."

"Surely not." I run my fingers over her shoulder.

"It is. And it means so much more because it's with you. How do you work that charm on me?" Her hand goes to my cheek, and she leans in, kissing me.

"I'm just that good."

"Yeah, you are," she says with a laugh.

The film starts, and she nuzzles up to me. I could get used to this life.

We watch the movie for the first forty minutes or so, but to be honest, it's a little boring.

She unsnaps a few buttons of my shirt, sliding her hand

through the space she created, her fingers weaving through my chest hair.

"Cold?" I ask.

"My hands are a little."

I place my hand over my shirt and her hand, but she unsnaps another button, her hand roaming over my chest. One by one, the snaps are undone, and her fingers run over my bare skin. My cock has taken notice and is beginning to strain against my jeans.

"Are you sure you're cold?" I can't hide the amusement from my voice.

She tilts her head, kissing my chin. "I'm a little bored to be honest. Who's playing the movie?"

I have a feeling I know why she's asking. "My friend Nick said he'd come back after it was over to close up. So, no one is around right now."

"Perfect," she says, excitement in her tone.

She pushes down the blanket and straddles my lap. "Let me properly thank you for a great date."

She kisses my forehead, her tits right in my face. I graze my hands over her ribs and take her tits in my hands, squeezing them. She moans as I knew she would. Apparently, they're really sensitive these days.

"You don't have to thank me," I say, loving the sprinkle of kisses she's landing on my face.

She moans again when I tweak her nipples through her dress. I swear she's trying to kill me by not wearing a bra. She slides down my body, undoing any snap she missed.

"What are you doing?" My voice is as gravelly as this parking lot.

It's obvious what she intends, and I'm not about to stop her. She's gone down on me a few times, but I always stop her before I come, unable to resist the urge to be inside her.

She slips down between my legs. "Do I really need to explain it to you?"

Her fingers hover over the button on my jeans, and I watch her unfasten it. My dick is hard, pressing against my zipper, and she gently lowers it, carefully going over my bulge. Then she sets her eyes on me, and the lust and desire pooled in them causes my hips to rise off the inflatable couch.

"Fuck, Briar."

She slides her hand inside my jeans, palming my length, rubbing and squeezing. "Have I told you how much I love your cock?"

"No, but I'd love to hear all about it."

Her hand pumps me through my black boxer briefs. "It's so thick and long and fits me perfectly."

I cradle her cheek. "Take it out, sweetheart."

She hooks her hands in the waistband of my jeans, and I lift my hips for her to drag them down to my ankles. I swallow hard when she runs her plump lips over the bulge, her nails scraping my stomach as she dips them under the waistband of my boxer briefs, dragging them up and over my dick, resting them under my balls.

The cool air hits my dick, but she wraps her hand around it, pumping, watching me. "I want to see you come undone."

My fingers weave through her hair, gripping the back of her head. "It won't take much."

She brings her lips to my tip, tongue sliding out and twirling, licking up the pre-cum that's already leaking out. Without warning, she opens her mouth and swallows me down her throat, holding my base firm.

"Damn," I say, my head falling back, eyes closing.

She draws my dick out of her mouth, her saliva dripping down my length. "Eyes on me, big guy."

I chuckle and watch her. I'm sure my eyes are hooded as she takes me into her mouth again. She works me over, twisting and tugging, tapping the tip on her tongue. I'm fixated, and every time her eyes swoop up to mine, my cock twitches in her mouth, and she smiles with her lips wrapped around me.

I'm lost in the world of Briar, and I don't want to be found.

"I'm gonna come." My ass inches up to get as far back in her throat as I can.

She pulls my dick out of her mouth and holds the tip right on her splayed tongue, waiting, and with a roar from deep in my throat, I empty myself in her mouth. She covers my tip with her lips and sucks gently until I've given her everything I can.

After my orgasm retreats and my ass is back on the inflatable couch, she cleans me up and slides my boxer briefs back up.

"C'mere." I place my hands under her arms and help her up off her knees. She straddles me, and I brush her hair away from her face. "Was it as good as you thought it would be?"

She jabs me in the shoulder. "Jackass."

I chuckle and bury my face in her neck. "Best blow job ever."

She giggles, and I roll us over, setting her back on the inflatable couch.

"And now it's your turn." I slide down her body.

When will I ever get enough of this woman?

Once the movie is done, we pack up and I drive us back to my place. My house that has become a home with the addition of Briar. I'm completely screwed if she ever leaves me.

Chapter Thirty

BRIAR

"Do we have to go?" Emmett wraps his arms around my waist, tugging me against him and away from the bathroom counter.

"I'm trying to get ready," I say, tilting my neck so he can kiss his way up to my ear.

He lightly bites my earlobe and sucks it. "Come back to bed."

"It's your brother's baby shower."

His hands fall to my stomach. "And yours will be next."

"I don't expect a shower."

He slides his hands to my hips and turns me around to face him, stepping into me so my back presses against the counter. "Everyone will want to celebrate this little one."

I'm not so sure. There are so many questions that wake me up at night. If I stay with Emmett, will the Noughtons accept my baby since he's not the father? They're all sweet and nice, but this circumstance is unusual. Then again, they've accepted Clayton as their own.

"Stop thinking so hard." He presses his lips to my collarbone. "You're putting too much stress on yourself, which can be solved by just telling Gillian."

I slide out of his arms, turning to the sink to continue putting on my makeup.

He sighs. "I'm just—"

"I know. I know. We're having lunch in Lincoln this week under the guise of it being a shopping trip. I'll tell her then. Far away from here where she'll have to ride back with me."

He slides up to sit on the counter, watching me. "I'd like to be there for you."

I side-eye him, putting on my eyeliner. "I think it's best that I do this alone."

"Cool." He pushes off the counter, goes to the shower, and turns it on.

"Emmett..." I sigh, knowing he's disappointed.

He's been making little comments here and there, and I think he's growing restless that we haven't told anyone.

He strips his boxers off and is about to get into the shower when I hug him from behind, pressing kisses along his spine.

"Don't be mad." I tighten my arms around him, and his hands cover my hands on his chest.

"I just feel like we're in a stall pattern until everyone knows. I thought sneaking around would be fun for a while, but it's not."

I squeeze him. "You're right. I can't today because I don't want to ruin Sadie and Jude's baby shower, but tonight. I'll tell her everything tonight." It's time I woman up and tell Gillian the truth. As it is, I have to face Chad at some point as well.

He swivels in my arms, takes my head in his hands, and kisses me thoroughly. "I think you'll feel better, and then you just have to concentrate on growing this little one."

"And we can focus on getting the dude ranch going for you. And we need to talk about that daddy shower thing. I think it could be a profitable endeavor. Along with the gender reveal parties. These are all ideas we need to sketch out into a business plan for you to present at that quarterly meeting you mentioned."

"Would you help me?"

"You don't even need to ask." I kiss his chest. "Now go clean up so we're not late."

"I'd rather get dirty with you." He pulls me into him, his hardening length pressing against my stomach.

It's so tempting, but if I'm telling Gillian tonight, then I need to make sure I'm on time for the shower. No sense starting off on the wrong foot by being late.

I push his chest. "Go."

"Later?" He cocks an eyebrow and opens the shower door.

"Is that even a question?"

He steps into the shower, and I go into my bedroom, which I'm never in anymore, and grab the flowy dress I plan to wear. I stare at myself in the mirror, turning to the side and examining my stomach. It's protruding a bit, but I'm sure to anyone else, it looks as though I ate a big meal. I run my hands over the tiny swell.

This thing with Emmett has been so wonderful. Who would've guessed that he'd be so forthcoming with his feelings? He's let me in completely. The only thing he hasn't talked about much is his brothers and the fight they had, but I know it bothers him.

We've barely been together for any real time at all, and I'm not naïve enough to think that with all the obstacles we're about to face, we'll for sure make it to the happily ever after stage, but I know he's worth the risk. He's worth the heartbreak if it ends up not working. I will be crushed, as my feelings for him are already so much more than I felt for Chad, but what if it does work? There's no chance I can walk away now and live with the what-ifs.

I look down at my stomach. "Regardless, it will always be me and you, and I promise you, I'm not going anywhere," I whisper.

There's a knock at the front door, and I walk out of my bedroom and peek into Emmett's. His towel is around his waist, and he's in his closet, getting clothes.

"I'll get it," I say.

"You should, it's your house." He laughs.

I shake my head and walk down the steps, seeing Scarlett standing on the porch. I open the door for her, and she smiles, but something about it seems off.

"I love your dress," I say.

"You too." Her dark hair is pulled half up with the rest in waves, and her dress is a pretty maroon with a small flower pattern. "Do you mind if I come in?"

"Of course." I open the door wider and step out of the way. "Emmett is just finishing getting ready, I think."

"I can wait until he's done."

"Do you want a drink?" I head into the kitchen.

"Sure, water would be great."

She stands at the island, and I dig out two waters from the fridge. Her eyes scour the area, concentrating on some papers on the table. Emmett's plans for the dude ranch. If she notices what they are, she doesn't say anything.

"Exciting day," I say.

"Definitely." She glances at the stairs. "Sorry to barge in on you guys before the shower."

I wave her off. "No need to apologize. Is everything okay?"

"Um...yeah. Just something came up that I wanted to talk to you and Emmett about before the shower."

My hand tightens around my drink, and I take another sip of water. "You're scaring me. Does it have to do with the yoga classes? There aren't enough people, right?"

She waves me off and shakes her head. "No. It's going

great, and we get rave reviews on your classes. Everyone loves you. I'm still trying to get more people there, but I think it will build over time. I planned for the classes not to be full at the beginning."

"I heard that Wild Bull Ranch is opening a spa," I say.

Scarlett scowls. "I hate Walker Matthews. Why would he start up a spa when he has the smallest B&B? I mean, come on, he can't compete with us. He's so cocky. Don't be surprised if I build a five thousand square foot spa just to one-up him."

I laugh and set my water on the counter as Emmett barrels down the stairs. He stops when he reaches Scarlett.

"Talking about Walker Matthews again?" He laughs, kissing his cousin on the cheek.

"The man drives me insane." She waves. "But I'm glad you're here. Can we sit?"

I glance at Emmett and his eyebrows furrow.

"What's up?" he asks.

Scarlett has always been super nice to me, but I don't know her well, so I'm hoping Emmett can decipher what I can't.

"Let's go into the family room." Emmett stands to the side, waiting for Scarlett to go first.

When I walk by, Emmett places his hand on the small of my back, leading me into the room. I step away as soon as Scarlett turns to sit in the chair.

She clasps her hands in her lap. "So, I got a call yesterday, and at first, I wasn't going to tell either of you about it because it's not really my business. I'm not like everyone else in this family who thinks that if it's a family member, we're entitled to know."

"Just spit it out, Scarlett," Emmett says.

"Do you know a woman named Parker?"

My body freezes, and my heart thumps loudly. Please say

it's another Parker and not the woman we met in the waiting room in Lincoln.

"Um..." Emmett says because I'm frozen.

Scarlett's eyes are on me.

"What do you know?" I ask, ready to face it. She clearly knows something. She wouldn't be here otherwise.

"Well, she called and said she was friends with Emmett and his *wife*. That she's been following your account, Emmett, and ran into you both at your OB appointment."

"Man, she just outed us completely in one swoop," Emmett says, sliding closer to me and putting his arm around my back.

Scarlett's eyes widen. "You're married?"

Emmett shakes his head. "No, but we're a couple."

"That just kind of came out while we were talking to Parker," I say. "Didn't want to have to explain the situation."

"But you're pregnant?" She looks at me with wide eyes.

How can I tell her without telling Gillian first? It feels like such a betrayal. Emmett found out by accident, but if I tell Scarlett right now, it's purposely telling someone before my sister and that doesn't feel right. But I have no one to blame except myself for putting it off for so long.

"I am," I say. "It's complicated."

I don't mention the baby's parentage, not wanting to get into it right now. Gillian should be the first to know the whole situation.

She raises her hand and shakes her head. "It's not my business. I'm sure you have plans to tell people, but this Parker said she was going to drive down here today to see the place. She really wants some gender reveal party like the one she saw online."

"She's coming here?" My stomach turns over, and my head whips toward Emmett.

"I stalled her. I said we had a big family get-together today and that no one would have time to talk to her. She said okay, and I scheduled for her to come next week, even though we don't have a gender reveal party package." Her gaze lands on Emmett, and he laughs.

"Well..."

"Is this the thing Ben's been trying to talk to me about?" She looks toward the kitchen table again. "Why haven't you come to me?"

I pat his leg. "I should leave you guys alone."

Emmett grabs my hand. "Stay. You're just as big a part of this as me. You made me see a bigger vision."

Scarlett smiles at her cousin, and her gaze flicks to our joined hands. She crosses her legs, putting her elbow on her knee and her chin in her palm. "Tell me, because this Parker woman couldn't stop going on and on about the gender reveal and some daddy shower for her husband. It sounds like something we should offer."

I turn toward Emmett, and his face lights up. My heart explodes for him.

For the next half hour, Emmett tells Scarlett all the ideas we've come up with and how he wants to run it. He wants to be in charge of the dude ranch part, and he turns to me. "I think Briar should be in charge of the other plans. Putting schedules together, arranging whatever is on the other end."

"No," I say, my head going from him to Scarlett. "This is your idea. Not mine."

"Not true. When Parker came up to us, Briar is the one who sold her on the daddy shower thing. And she's had other ideas too."

Scarlett stares at me for a second. I'm ready for her to tell me I'm just a yoga instructor, but she leans forward and pats my leg. "Come see me in my office on Monday morning."

"But—"

"And you have my vote, Emmett. I'll stand by your side during the meeting."

A rush of air leaves Emmett. "Shit, Scarlett, I don't know what to say."

"That you should've come to me sooner?" She raises her eyebrows, and I laugh. "Now stand up and let me give you each a hug." I stand, and she squeezes me tightly. "Congratulations. I knew he'd find someone who could handle him. He's really a softy, isn't he?"

She laughs and walks over to Emmett. When she pulls away from their hug, Scarlett looks back at me. "Your secret is safe with me, but the family would be very happy to have you as a part of it. You practically are already. And I know Gillian has been a little overbearing lately, but she knows deep down that Emmett will take care of you. Trust her." She steps toward the door. "See you guys in a little bit."

We wave, and she shuts the door.

I blow out a breath. "Did that actually happen?"

"I was gonna ask you the same thing."

"I'm sorry I didn't tell her the baby isn't yours. I just... Gillian should know first."

"Don't sweat it." Emmett's arms swoop in and pick me up. "After you tell Gillian tonight, we'll finally be released from these chains, and we can just be us."

He swings me around, but all I can think is that telling my sister could be the start of a lot of problems for us. I'm not so sure Scarlett is right. But I sure hope she is.

Chapter Thirty-One

EMMETT

I sit in the back of The Knotted Barn, watching Sadie ooh and aah over all her gifts. Gillian has had Briar next to her since we walked in together, and Scarlett keeps giving me this knowing smile. Ben is ignoring me, both of our black eyes barely visible anymore, and Jude sits next to Sadie, looking disgruntled as always.

The more I sit here watching them open gifts, the more bitter I become. Everyone in this room should know I'm with Briar. That we've found that something special together. Sure, I'll deal with the shitty comments about how they never thought they'd see the day and I'm not mature enough to be in a serious relationship. They'll all cast their judgments on me, but I don't give a shit because Briar sees the real me. She knows who I really am under my jokester exterior.

Bennett folds himself into the seat next to me, eyeing Briar. "So did you take the step?"

"What?"

He leans in closer. "You know what I'm asking."

I shouldn't tell anyone. Scarlett knows, and Bennett

knows that I was entertaining the idea. But if Briar's telling Gillian tonight, does it really matter if Bennett knows?

I nod.

He smiles. "I'm proud of you."

"Because it turns out I was wrong about all the shit I used to say?"

He chuckles. "Yeah. But you took a chance. It's hard to do that. I struggle with it myself." He nods at Wren sitting in front of Sadie, taking each bow or ribbon and putting it in her lap. "She needs a mom, a woman in her life, but I just can't do it. I can't take that step."

The day Bennett buried Kristie, I didn't know what to say. I looked at Darla holding Wren, and I knew exactly what that little girl would miss having in her life. She would only know her mother through stories. I'm nothing like a mother, but I try to be a constant in Wren's life. Her family dynamic might be different than others, but she's loved. Wholeheartedly. I don't ever want her to question that.

Getting closer to Wren helped heal me in a way. It healed the pain I'd always felt because I don't remember my mom when both my brothers have their memories of her. My mom didn't choose to leave. She was taken from us. Just like Kristie was taken from Wren. Aunt Darla and Aunt Bette try to fill that role for Wren. And my dad did a bang-up job of trying to be both for my brothers and me. We were loved. Nothing I could do would ever bring my mom back, so I needed to be grateful because though I didn't have a mom, I had the rest of my family.

"Maybe you're not ready," I say to him.

"It's been six years."

Wren looks over her shoulder, finds her dad, and smiles. He returns her smile, though it's edged with pain.

"Then maybe you just haven't met the one yet."

He chuckles. "So, you believe in soul mates now?"

I shake my head. "Nah, because then Kristie would've been yours."

"She was." There's a depression in his voice I haven't heard in a few years. I think it's why Wren is all about Briar—she's looking for someone to fill that role, and he knows it. But Bennett isn't ready to find someone who could fit into their lives.

"Whoever the lucky woman is who will get to help raise Wren, you just haven't found her yet."

His eyes wander away from Wren and zero in on my dad. "Maybe I'll end up like your dad."

I shake my head. "You're no Bruce." I can't picture Bennett having a different woman in his bed every Saturday night. "Maybe join a group or a club or something. Go out to more places than The Hidden Cave."

He looks at me and leans in a bit. "That reminds me. There was a note on The Canary Wall the other day about you renting out Nick's drive-in for a night to take a woman there. Was it really you, or is it bullshit?"

My gut twists and my eyes focus on the back of Briar's head. I nod.

"And?"

I nod again.

"Well then, I think I should tell you, you're gonna be outed soon. Melvin was in the bathroom, so I wrote a note with a bullshit story about Louise from the county clerk's office and Mr. Torres hiding out in one of the library study rooms."

My eyebrows raise. "You lied?"

He rocks his head back and forth. "Technically it's true, but I don't think anything was going on. But he did have to fix his ponytail after coming out. Wren was waiting for story time to start. Anyway, I put my notecard over the one that was talking about you."

"Thanks, man."

He shrugs. "You'll do the same for me one day."

"Promise."

Briar gets up from her chair and heads to the hallway where the bathrooms are located. This is my opportunity.

"Do me one more favor?" I ask.

"Go."

I slide out of my chair and head toward the bathroom hallway. Briar isn't there, so I assume she's already in the women's bathroom.

I push the door open and peek my head in. "Briar?"

I find her at the sink, blotting her face with a paper towel. She's fucking crying. My chest squeezes.

"What's going on?" I rush over to her, not worrying about if anyone comes in. I wrap my arms around her, pulling her toward me, running my hand over her hair, trying to soothe her as she cries into my shirt. I hope it's just hormones or something. "What's wrong?"

She pulls away a little. "I'm going to be a horrible mother. I don't know what any of that stuff is." I laugh, and her eyes narrow. "It's not funny. Did you see that breast pump? I'm supposed to put those on my nipples and let them suck the milk out? It's horrifying."

"Would you rather I milk you? It's a chore, but I'll do it for you." I shrug.

She pushes me on the shoulder and shakes her head. "Not funny."

"It's kind of funny." I try to make her smile, but she's not having it.

"And all that stuff... how am I going to afford all that stuff?"

"You're going to have a baby shower."

She circles out of my arms. "No one will want to celebrate my baby. Sadie and Jude have loved each other their entire lives. The whole town of Willowbrook is on cloud nine in there. I'm pregnant with a jackass's baby, and he doesn't even know I'm pregnant. People are going to think..." She doesn't finish her sentence.

My head cocks to the side. "Think?"

Her eyes meet mine through the mirror. "You know."

"I don't."

"That I tricked you into this relationship to help me raise my baby because I have nothing. And no one. I love being a yoga instructor, but let's be real, the pay can't support me and a baby. People will say I trapped you."

I lean against the counter so I can look directly in her eyes and not through a mirror. "It's not my baby, so did you trap me?"

She throws up her arms and drills me with a death glare. She knows I have a point. "You know this town. You know I'll be crucified. I saw what happened to my sister when she got pregnant. I just happen to return, move in with you, and suddenly you're in lo—you like me."

A smile tips my lips. "Sorry, what?"

"You know... that you like me."

"Love you," I clarify.

She tears her eyes away. "That was a slip-up."

I wrap my arm around her waist and tug her to me. "So, you think I love you?"

"No," she grumbles.

I dip my head down to meet her eyes. "That's a shame."

She says nothing, and I place my finger under her chin, bringing it up so she has no choice but to look into my eyes.

"Because I do. I love you, Briar."

A shuddering breath leaves her. "No, you don't."

She wiggles out of my hold, but I grab her wrist. "Are you trying to tell me what I feel, sweetheart?"

"I need some air." She pulls away from my grip and walks out of the bathroom.

I follow, and she pushes out the door of the hallway that leads directly outside, the sun casting down on her like a vision. She heads around the corner, not wanting to be seen.

"So, you don't love me?" I ask.

"I..." Her mouth opens and closes a few times before she turns away from me.

"Fair enough. It seems I have more work to do. I'm happy to take on the job." I go to her back, hugging her from behind. "We have *this,* Briar. I know you feel it too. We're a we. A pair. It's petrifying and some people are gonna talk shit, but we're stronger together." I cradle her stomach. "I know this baby isn't biologically mine, but I will love it as my own. Even if we don't work out and years down the road you discover I'm not the one you want, I'm still going to be a part of this child's life. I will never abandon him or her. I promise you that."

"Emmett," she says softly, leaning her head on my shoulder.

"I'm serious, Briar. Nightly feedings? Sign me up. Putting a crib together? I'm your guy. Diaper explosions? Well... you might have to take those." She laughs, and I squeeze her tighter against me. "I love you and the baby. It's scary that things are moving fast, I know, but I don't think you can deny that what we have is different than anything we've ever had with anyone else."

"I know," she whispers.

I run my nose up and down her neck. "Repeat after me."

"Emmett..."

"Emmett loves Briar."

She shakes her head.

"Say it," I urge her.

She swivels in my arms, bringing her hands up and around my neck. She stares into my eyes. "Briar loves Emmett."

All the air in my lungs rushes out.

She giggles. "I love making you speechless."

"Is that the truth?" I hold my breath, waiting for her answer.

She nods. "I love you, Emmett. As much as that scares me, along with all the unknowns in front of us, I love you, and you're the man I want to share all of this with."

"What's around here?" a woman says.

Briar turns away from me, glancing over her shoulder.

"Hey, you two! Fancy meeting you here." Parker walks toward us in a sundress and heels, her purse hanging off her arm. "Baby, come meet the guy from the video and his beautiful wife."

"Wife?" Ben's voice comes from behind me.

Pop. There goes our bubble.

Chapter Thirty-Two

BRIAR

I dislodge from Emmett's hold, and the disappointment that flashes across his face is hard to witness.

"Parker? What are you doing here?" I ask the woman who was told not to come here today but decided to barge in anyway.

"I brought my hubby to see the place. I talked to um… a Scarlett, and she told me you had a family thing, but we had the babysitter booked already and wanted to take a little day trip, so I said let's go see Plain Daisy Ranch. I could show him the lay of the land and the other businesses even if we couldn't talk to anyone today." She hooks her arm through her husband's, and for the first time, I look at him.

I stumble back, grabbing Emmett's arm, and my entire body goes numb.

Chad is dressed how I remember, though I never realized the stark difference between him and Emmett until now that they're standing feet away from one another. His shirt is tucked into his slacks with a belt, and his head doesn't hold one wayward hair. The loafers he's wearing are what he considers casual Sunday wear.

I feel Emmett's eyes on me, but I'm frozen in place. This cannot be happening right now.

Emmett takes over the conversation as I try to recover from my shock. "Yeah, Scarlett told us that you were coming later this week," he says.

Parker waves. "Hubby can't come next week." Her gaze falls to Emmett then Ben. "This is the guy you think you can compete with."

Parker laughs, and my eyes widen because she has no idea what she really just said.

"If you'll excuse me," I say, turning and running right into Ben.

He grabs my arms to stop me and looks down at me with concern. "What's going on?"

I shake my head, and he releases me, seeing the tears filling my eyes.

"Don't you hate that about pregnancy? The nausea comes when you least expect it," Parker says.

Ben's vision locks with Emmett's over my head.

"Pregnant?" Ben steps around me, fury transforming his face.

"Ben, have you seen—" Gillian stops in her tracks. "There you are." She looks at me and then at everyone else. Her forehead creases, not knowing what's going on. "Oh, hi."

"Wait." Parker points at Ben. "You're that football player."

"Ben Noughton," Gillian says proudly and smiles. "And you are?"

"Parker. Parker Hemmons."

Nausea churns my stomach.

"Nice to meet you. Are you a friend of Sadie and Jude's?" Gillian looks at Ben as if he might recognize them.

"No. I met Briar"—she points at me—"and Emmett at the doctor's office. I saw the video of the gender reveal and wait..." Her eyes light up. "Is the thing today for Sadie and Jude?" She says it as if she knows them. "Is that the family party going on?"

Gillian steps closer and glances over her shoulder at me. "Did you say doctor's office?"

"Why is everyone out here?" Jude steps out and joins us. "The presents are done, thank God. Now you jackasses have to help me take them to the house." He draws back when he notices Parker and Chad. "Who are you?"

"Parker, and this is my husband, Chad." She rests her hand on her swollen belly. "Is there a bathroom here? This baby just loves to sit right on my bladder." She walks toward me as if I'm going to show her, which is probably the best idea right now because she's about to become collateral damage.

Lottie steps out of the building and draws back. "Is the party moving out here now?"

"Excuse me, can you point me to the bathroom?" Parker asks when none of the rest of us answer her.

"Right through the doors on your right." Lottie points at the doors she just came out of. "What's going on?"

"Who are these people, and what doctor's appointment were you at?" Gillian asks, stepping up in front of me.

"I, um..."

"You better be fucking kidding me, Emmett." Ben steps toward him, and I try to step away. I can't deal with all of this right now.

"What?" Gillian stiffens. "What's going on?"

Emmett holds up his hands. "It just happened." He steps back. "I love her, man."

"You love her," Chad says, his gaze shooting my way.

Gillian looks from Ben to me. Maybe putting the pieces together, but I don't know.

Lottie steps over to stand next to me, her hand going to my arm.

"You love her? Are you kidding me?" Ben shouts. "We had

a deal! And you go off and get her pregnant?" Ben cocks his fist back.

Jude grabs Ben's arm, stopping him. "I'm done with this shit. We're brothers. We have each other's backs."

Emmett steps to the side, and Ben yanks his arm from Jude's hold.

"Briar? What is he talking about?" Gillian asks.

I meet her eyes, my own stinging with tears.

Ben erupts in fake laughter. "While we thought they were just roommates, it turns out they fell in love, and now Briar is pregnant with Emmett's baby."

"What?" Gillian screeches, gripping my upper arms. Tears well in her eyes. "Why didn't you tell me?"

"Sorry, Jude. I love you, Emmett, but you need to grow the fuck up." Ben tackles Emmett to the ground, and they look just like they did on the softball field, rolling around and straddling one another, punching the other.

"Stop!" I shout, unable to see them at odds because of me.

Surprisingly, they do, and Emmett hops off Ben, fixing his shirt.

"What the hell is going on?" Bruce comes out along with Sadie, Clayton, and everyone else in the family.

Just fucking great.

"Hey, did you know there's some lady in the bathroom talking on the phone?" Romy asks.

"The baby isn't Emmett's," I spit it out before I lose my nerve.

I step out in front of everyone. My eyes turn to Chad, and his mouth hangs open, his shock and panic evident.

"Who is the father?" Gillian asks.

"It doesn't matter. He doesn't know. But..." I step over to Emmett and link my hand with his. "I love Emmett. I know how you feel." I raise my chin and keep my eyes on Gillian. "That you were so scared he was going to hurt me, but..." I look up at Emmett and the love that shines in his eyes. "He won't. He's kind and supportive and funny, and I've fallen head over heels in love with him. And if you have a problem with it, then I'm sorry because he's the one I've chosen."

Emmett unlocks our hands and pulls me into his side, kissing my temple. "I'm proud of you."

I close my eyes and remind myself that everything will be okay because Emmett has my back.

"But..." Gillian steps forward, and I pull away from Emmett to look at her. "This whole time you've been back... you've hidden this from me? I thought..." Tears stream down her face. "I'm sorry." She shakes her head. "I thought I was protecting you."

"I know. I know you did, and that's why I didn't want to disappoint you. I was scared to tell you, but if I'd just been honest, we wouldn't be here."

Gillian shakes her head. "No, it's my fault."

"You did go a little crazy," Emmett says, and I hit him in the stomach. "I mean, I love you, Gilly Bean."

Gillian hugs me—so tight and accepting. "I'm sorry. I never should've acted the way I did. But you should know that Clayton is the best thing in my life, and this little one is going to be yours. And I'm going to be supportive. I promise."

"Well, this is all well and good, but I'd like to talk to Briar if I could?"

My body stills when Chad speaks.

Gillian releases me and turns around. "And who are you?"

Emmett comes to my side, and I look up at him. I know he had an inkling when I froze earlier when Chad came around the corner.

"What's your name again?" Emmett asks him.

"Chad. Chad Hemmons." Chad has the audacity to step forward with his hand out. I guess when you're a secretive fuck, you think everyone else is too. Chad probably assumes

Emmett doesn't know who he is. "Parker just said that Briar was the one with all the plans about the gender reveal, and I don't have a lot of time, so I wanted to speak with her to get this going."

"It's scary how fast you can come up with your lies," I say.

"Briar?" Emmett asks, and his question is clear.

I nod.

Emmett steps up to Chad, cocking his fist back, and punches him square in the jaw.

Chad stumbles back, almost falling, holding his cheek. Obviously realizing the jig is up, he scowls at Emmett. "You're punching me after she fucked me and is now lying and saying that the baby is mine? It's not mine. Who knows how many men she slept with?"

Gillian steps up to Emmett's side, but Ben pushes her back, coming shoulder-to-shoulder with Emmett. "Get the fuck off our property."

Jude steps up so he's on Emmett's other side. I can see a part of Emmett knit back together when his brothers have his back.

"You're on your own," Chad says to me. "Don't try to get child support from me."

Gillian pushes through the two brothers and uses both hands to push Chad farther down the walkway. "She doesn't need you. She has all of us. And I bet your wife doesn't know what a slimeball you are. We don't want your money or empty promises."

I move to join Gillian. Emmett tries to keep me back, but I stand with my sister. "You're a piece of shit. You played me for a fucking year. Told me lie after lie. You don't want this baby? That's fine, I don't want you to be his or her father. I don't need your money, and I don't need you."

Bruce steps forward now. "I suggest you get outta here before I grab my shotgun and start shooting trespassers."

Parker comes back out of the building. "Whoa, sorry, my BFF is going through... what happened?" She runs toward Chad. "Oh my god, what happened?"

"I'm gonna sue you. What kind of place are you running here? The bastard punched me."

Parker looks back at us, horrified. "Why would you do that?"

"Ask him," Emmett says, nodding at Chad.

Chad walks off like the coward he is while Parker's eyes ping back and forth between us all, trying to figure out what happened while she was in the bathroom and on the phone. Eventually she joins her husband, walking down the hill toward their expensive SUV.

I go over to Emmett and look at his hand. "Let's get you some ice."

I don't wait for anyone else to say anything, leading him inside The Knotted Barn.

"Why does everything happen here?" Romy says, shaking her head and following us inside.

Everyone comes back in, and one of the servers gets me a bag of ice.

I sit Emmett in a chair and hold the ice on his hand. "Well, it's all out now."

He gives me a tender smile. "It's out. You guys okay?" His gaze dips to my stomach.

I place my free hand on it. "We're great."

"I hate to do this, but I need the two of you," Bruce interrupts.

Emmett looks up at his dad and nods as if he knows what his dad wants, but I have no idea.

Emmett stands and hands his bag of ice to Ben. "Ice your eye."

"Fucker, it just healed." Ben accepts the ice and puts it on his eye.

Eight of us walk out of The Knotted Barn. Bruce; Ben, Gillian, and Clayton; Jude and Sadie; and Emmett and I get into the UTVs. We drive until we reach the hill covered in daisies.

"Let's go visit Mom," Bruce says, and we all follow the trail up the hill.

Chapter Thirty-Three

EMMETT

As soon as my dad came up to Briar and me after the huge fight that broke out at yet another family gathering, I knew he'd reached his limit. His sons have brawled twice now, and I'm sure he knows we haven't been talking.

We all stand at the base of the hill covered in daisies, and my dad turns and faces us. "Now, I want you all to know, this is usually done on horseback, but what with the two of you being pregnant, I wouldn't risk it. But be prepared for next time."

Clayton walks with Dad, and the rest of us pair up in birth order. Jude and Sadie, Ben and Gillian, and Briar and me pulling up the rear. I hold her hand, wanting to comfort her. Emotions run high at these meetings. While I usually take the comedic route, my feet are on the coals this time.

Dad opens the gate and walks through to the family plot, holding the gate open for Clayton. We all file in, and I shut it behind me.

Dad walks up to my mom's headstone first. "Hey Daisy, the boys are at it again, but we have exciting news." He kisses his fingers and presses them to the stone. "This is Ben and Gillian's boy, Clayton. He's a first-timer." He nods at Clayton. "Say hi to Grandma Daisy."

"Hi," Clayton says, touching his fingers to the top of the tombstone.

He stands off next to Dad.

Jude steps up with Sadie. "Hey, Mom. I knew better. You taught me better. I'm sorry. We had the shower today, and we were spoiled rotten. Wish you were here to see your first granddaughter, Daisy." Jude kisses his fingers and places them on the headstone, stepping aside so Sadie can say something.

"Hi, Mrs. Noughton. We miss you, and we'll tell Daisy amazing stories about her namesake." Tears fall from Sadie's face onto the headstone.

Ben goes next. "Hey, Mom. Yeah, I have a black eye. It's my second one from Emmett in three weeks." He glances over his shoulder at me with narrowed eyes. "You remember Gillian? We're getting married in a few months. Can't wait to finally make her my wife." He does the same thing as my dad and Jude, kissing his fingers and touching the top of her headstone.

I bring Briar up by the hand and stare at my mom's name etched in the stone, my chest painfully tight. "This is Briar, Mom. I know… you're as shocked as anyone else that I'm in love, but she blew into my life, and I was lucky enough to catch her. Thankfully, she loves me too. And she's pregnant. The baby isn't mine by blood, but they are in my heart. I'll raise him or her no different than I would my own. I've been keeping secrets from the family, which is probably the reason we're all here." I bend down and kiss the top of her headstone.

We both step to the side.

"Even as adults, Daisy, they're fighting like cubs." My dad shakes his head. "Tackling one another, punching each other. It's embarrassing. I thought I raised them right."

"Come on, Dad," Jude says. "We weren't that bad."

"Yes, you were. It was on The Canary Wall. And I had to hear it down at Bingo Friday night. How, in the middle of a softball game, two of my sons couldn't handle their tempers. We're a family, and I brought all of you"—he scans the area—"up here because our family has grown. I'm blessed to have the women you love treat you so well. That you've each found your person, like I did with your mom. But now it's time that you all set your shit aside and get along."

"They think I'm stupid," I blurt. "That I can't handle the ranch."

Dad looks at Jude, then at me. "Emmett, I've always allowed you to be laidback, goofy, funny. I let you distract everyone with jokes and a good time, but you haven't been as responsible on the ranch as you could be. I blame myself. Jude took to the ranch quick, and he loved it. Ben left to play football. And you, I just let you be. You never said you wanted to leave Willowbrook, so I assumed that one day you and Jude would run this place together. But I see now that I never let you find your passion like your brothers did."

I always figured I'd find that love too. That one day, I'd just enjoy being a rancher. Herding cattle and planting corn. That if I did it long enough, that feeling of pride after a hard day's work would come. But it never has.

"Someone helped me get to your videos on my phone, and I watched them. Of course they're getting views," Dad says. "I see how naturally it comes to you."

"You mean showing off?" Ben grumbles.

"Ben, I wish you would've guided him more," Dad calls him out.

I want to grin at my brother, but I don't because I know I'll get shit for it if I do.

"I'm being blamed?" Ben thumbs at himself.

"You got the opportunity to live out your dream. I'm

surprised you never saw how unhappy Emmett was either. That he wasn't living up to his full potential because he was miserable."

"I'm the one who told him I'd get him the votes if..." His attention moves to Briar.

Gillian looks from him to me and back. "What?"

I turn to Briar. "Whatever is about to happen, just hear me out, okay?"

She inhales deeply, but her hand stays locked in mine.

Ben says, "I made a deal with Emmett that I'd help him get the votes at the quarterly meeting for a dude ranch if he..."

"If he what, Ben?" Gillian asks.

"If he stayed away from Briar."

A rush of air whooshes out of Briar, but she doesn't say anything.

I squeeze her hand and turn to her, shielding her from my family. "It was before anything went down with us. When you hated me. I promise."

Dad laughs and shakes his head. "You guys are morons." He looks at Gillian and Ben. "You practically pushed them together. I mean, I did my job, but you two acting like they were committing incest if they got together just drove them even closer together. They probably bonded over your obsession to try to keep them apart."

"Wait, Dad. You did your part?" My head tilts.

He laughs and claps Clayton on the back. "Briar moving in with you. Darla having Briar report for work at breakfast time when I knew you'd be there. Even Wren did her part, although she didn't know it. She just needed to show Briar you aren't the guy you pretend to be."

"Why would you do that?" Briar asks quietly.

"Because my boys tend to get in their own way sometimes. Daisy was my one. She's the only woman I'll ever love. You boys give me hell for my Saturday night visitors, and it probably wasn't the best example for you guys, but no one will ever replace your mom for me. That's why I haven't ever bothered to try. Now I look around this family meeting, and it makes me happy and proud that you've each found your person. My advice is to hold on tight and enjoy the ride for as long as you have one another. And stop fighting with your damn brothers." He eyes each one of us. "Emmett, you have my vote at the meeting. You're a different person in those videos. Scarlett talked to me earlier about the other plans you and Briar have. I think it can be profitable."

"Thanks, Dad." I have to swallow the lump forming in my throat.

He turns to Jude. "Emmett isn't gonna take on more at the ranch. Train Nash. He can handle it."

Jude nods and then looks over at me. "I'm sorry for what I said that day. I don't think you're stupid, or any of that other shit. I'm just stressed with the baby coming, and it's maddening sometimes how you always seem so unstressed. I was your protector after Mom died, and pushing you and being hard on you felt like my role to get you to reach your full potential. But I see what Dad's saying. You're meant for a different role. I don't want to fight with you guys. With Daisy coming soon, I want her to see healthy relationships in her family."

"Thanks for being my protector growing up. Sometimes I'm so envious of you guys for having memories of Mom because I don't have any."

Briar steps closer to me. Her other hand wraps around my bicep, and she kisses my shoulder.

"We should talk about you more, Daisy," Dad says. "I'm sorry for that. Sometimes it's still so painful."

"I'm sorry too," Ben says to me. "But hey, aren't you glad I taught you how to punch? My eye is still stinging."

Everyone laughs.

"I love you, brother. Always," Ben says, and I swear his eyes look kind of glossy. "Dad's right. I should've known if something happened with you and Briar that you wouldn't ever hurt her intentionally. You're a lucky woman, Briar. I think I hopped on the crazy train with Gillian, just wanting to make sure she wasn't upset."

"Hey now," Gillian says.

"Mom..." Clayton cringes as though he's telling her to own it.

"Okay, yeah, I was a tad overprotective. But I knew someone had hurt you before you moved here, and I didn't want someone else to have the chance to. I'm sorry, Emmett, I love you, but I knew she had that crush on you in high school, and that's all I could think of when she was moving in with you."

"What?" Briar asks, mouth hanging open.

"Do you think I didn't see the notebooks? I packed that box for you to take when you left for Chicago. It wasn't much of a secret, except maybe from Emmett."

Briar covers her face with her hands. "This is so embarrassing."

I tug her into my chest. "It's okay, you scored your crush. You won."

She shakes her head and groans.

"Us Noughton boys are hard to resist. Sadie crushed on me for years," Jude says, puffing out his chest.

"And you me," she says, elbowing him.

"You should all be grateful to have one another. So now that we're all made up, the next time we come up here, it better be to celebrate something good." Dad steps up to Mom's tombstone.

The Noughton men circle around it, linking arms and staring at the top.

"Love you," we say in unison.

Then, as a family, we walk back to the UTVs, all of us silent. Briar doesn't seem upset about the deal I made with Ben, but I have a feeling I have some groveling to do when we get home. Which I'm more than happy to do between her legs. No complaints from me.

Chapter Thirty-Four

BRIAR

"Fuck," Emmett says, driving his hips up off the bed as I ride him.

"Oh my god, it feels so good."

He slides his hand down between us and toys with my clit. I rock back on him, my hands on his thighs, giving him all the access he needs. He takes me to the edge as he always does.

"Come for me, sweetheart," he says.

I slam down, and he grunts, his chest rising off the mattress. I fall forward, my hands on either side of his head.

"That's it. Right there." I take the control I need, using his finger for the friction I need on my clit.

My orgasm hits me hard and fast, and I collapse on him, but he rolls me over, putting one of my legs on his shoulder, and drills into me so deep I gasp.

"Fuck, I-love-you-so-much," he says as if it's all one word.

It's a common confession he makes when we're having sex.

He pumps in and out of me before he curses and lets some of his weight bear down on me. But he quickly rolls away, still afraid he might hurt the baby. We both lie on our backs, staring at the ceiling, breathing hard.

"Let me drive you," he says, not taking my previous nos for an answer.

I face him, propping my head on my palm. "This is a good thing for Gillian and me to do together. Plus, Parker isn't going to want a man around. Sorry."

He runs his hand over my cheek. "I hope she believes you."

"Me too, but I would want to know. It's not like he had a one-night stand. Looking back, I'm sure I wasn't the first woman he had an affair with, and I probably won't be the last. Plus, I want to give this one an opportunity to know her siblings someday. I mean, technically Gillian and I are only half siblings, but it's never felt any different with her than it does with Koa."

"Are you nervous about the lunch?"

I draw in a deep breath. "Yeah. Gillian pulled some strings by using Ben's name to get us a private area in a restaurant. I didn't want to go to Parker's house because what if Chad showed up?"

"I trust Gillian to protect you."

I laugh and straddle him. "Second only to you." I bend down and kiss him briefly before sliding off him. "Shower time."

I turn on the water, pee, and undo my ponytail that looks like most of Wren's if I'm honest. I shower, surprised Emmett doesn't join me as he usually does. Then I get dressed and ready to make the drive up to Lincoln to tell Parker about Chad.

My stomach is a ball of knots, but I keep reminding myself that I would want to know. I'm only telling her the truth. She can do with the information what she wants.

"Are you going to lie in bed all day?"

He sets his computer on my side of the bed. "I'm behaving myself, okay? I gave you time to get ready without being all over you. But I'm probably going to beat off when you leave."

I laugh. "Why? I'll be home tonight. And we just had sex. Literally."

"It's my way of controlling myself with you."

I sit on the edge of the bed, putting on my sandals. "Are you telling me you beat off just as much as before we got together?"

"Probably more honestly."

I shake my head. "You're always full of surprises, aren't you, Emmett Noughton?"

I stand and bend to kiss him goodbye. He holds my face to his mouth, sliding his tongue through the seam of my lips, and I sink down on his lap. I keep thinking I'll wake up, and we'll be one of those couples who never have sex. And maybe when the baby comes it will happen, but I can't imagine a time I don't look at Emmett and get turned on.

I pull away. "I gotta go."

"Okay, hurry back, and don't worry if you see a black truck following you on the highway."

I push his chest, and he falls back to the mattress. "And Ben will be with you?"

"Probably." He shrugs.

"I secretly love it, you know that, right?"

"I do. It's my job to know that." He touches the small swell of my belly. "Go before I chain you to the bed."

I step back toward the door. "Love you."

"Love you more."

I walk down the stairs, finding Gillian already on the porch. I open our front door, staring at the framed picture of the ultrasound right under one of Emmett and me by the lake that's on the wall.

"What are you doing? Why didn't you knock?" I ask.

"I'm cool with you two and all, but I don't want to hear you going at it. And I don't want to see Emmett naked." She has a whole-body shiver. "Ready?"

I grab my purse. "Yeah."

She takes my hand and squeezes it. "It's going to be fine. You're doing the right thing. Please remember that no matter what her reaction is, you aren't at fault here."

"Thanks for doing this with me."

She tightens her grip on my hand. "We're sisters."

"Yeah, we are."

We smile at one another. There's still some sadness in her eyes. I think she feels guilty for how protective she was and the fact that I didn't feel I could tell her about what I was going through.

We drive up to Lincoln, and Gillian valets her new SUV outside the lunch place. Standing on the sidewalk, staring at the sign and knowing Parker might be there, makes all the nausea that dissipated on the ride reappear.

"Come on." Gillian walks in first, telling the hostess we're here under a reservation.

We're taken to a small room that is roped off for privacy, and Parker sits at a table facing the doorway. She doesn't stand and doesn't look all that thrilled to see us. But she did agree to this meeting, so there's that.

"Hi, Parker. You remember my sister, Gillian?" I say, taking my seat.

"Yes, hello." She straightens her back, repositioning herself.

"Hi." Gillian sits down on the other side of Parker.

"The daddy shower thing is never going to happen now. Chad would never go there again. I'm not sure why you wanted to meet with me, but I hope it's to apologize."

I lean back in my chair. "I understand. There's something I want to tell you, and I wanted to do it face to face, so I'm glad you agreed to meet me."

Gillian nods.

Parker looks nervously between the two of us. "Your family is really dramatic, just so you know. Spit it out."

"I'm pregnant, but Emmett isn't the father." I press my hand to my stomach, trying to get my nerves under control.

She stills. "And that involves me how?" she asks, but her body language isn't as defensive as her words.

"I recently moved back to Willowbrook. I used to live in Chicago, but I went through a really bad break-up and moved home. Shortly before my move, I realized I was pregnant, and it was my previous boyfriend's baby."

Her demeanor shifts from defensive to something softer, more vulnerable. "Keep going." She lifts the sparkling water she must have ordered before we got here to her lips, and I notice that her hand is shaking a bit.

"The guy I was dating turned out to be married with kids. I never knew. He told me he lived in Chicago but traveled a lot for work and that was why he was out of town so much. I believed him. I had no reason not to. He was in hospitality, so it seemed legit. One night we were at my apartment, and I woke up in the middle of the night. The bathroom door was shut, but there was light coming out from under it. I thought maybe he wasn't feeling well, and when I went to check on him, I heard his voice through the door."

"Just tell me." Tears gather in her eyes, but I don't want to just spit it out. I want her to understand the situation.

"He was telling someone he'd be home tomorrow. That he was sorry they'd had such a hard day, and that he'd make it up to them when he got home. He said to book a babysitter and he'd plan a date night. That he was sorry he'd missed their wedding anniversary, but she couldn't have all those things she liked without him working. And him working meant him traveling."

Parker's hand shakes even more as she reaches for her glass again. "And who was the guy, Briar?" she whispers.

"I think you know." My gaze shifts to Gillian, who nods. "I didn't know Chad was your husband until the day you showed up on the ranch. I swear."

She takes a sip from her glass but tips the glass farther and farther back until she finishes it. "That's why I agreed to meet you. He told me that Emmett hit him because I forced him to go to the ranch when they told me not to come that day. He blamed me for getting punched, but I saw your face." Tears swim in her eyes. "Sure, there have been signs over the years, but he always made me feel like I was crazy. That I was purposely looking for something bad between us when we were happy. I've been with him since freshman year in college. We have three kids, and this one on the way." She runs her hand over her stomach, eyeing my barely-there bump. "Oh god, they're related."

"I'm sorry." My voice shakes.

She nods. "I need to go." She stands and grabs her purse.

"Wait, I—"

She stops at the opening of the room. "I know it took a lot to come to me, so thank you. And I believe you. Don't think I don't. I just need... time. My entire life just imploded, and I have to piece myself together because when I get home, there are three kids, not including this one, who need me. They come first, always. But..." Her gaze falls to my stomach once more. "I'll be in touch."

She leaves, and the tears that threatened to fall drip down my cheeks.

Gillian slides into Parker's chair and puts her arm around me, letting me cry on her shoulder. "It's okay. I know. It's emotional for everyone, but"—she draws back to meet my gaze—"he did this. To both of you. Neither of you are to blame, and I know you feel like the other woman, but you weren't because you didn't know. You thought you were the only woman. So, don't blame yourself for her pain. You didn't cause it, he did."

I nod, but I still feel like complete shit for what she has to go through.

"Now, we're going to have a nice lunch and..." She chuckles and looks toward the doorway.

Emmett walks through with Ben right behind him.

"What the?" I look at Gillian.

"I'm a big enough person to know that you need him right now, so I told them to drive up. I knew that poor woman wasn't going to have lunch with us. Now the four of us can get to know one another as couples. Jude and Sadie wanted to come, but Jude's all paranoid about her being too far from the hospital."

I hug Gillian. "Thank you."

She pats my back. "I'm sorry. I'll never fail you again."

I squeeze her tightly, and when she releases me, I step into Emmett's arms, the tears falling more steadily now.

He tucks his face into my neck. "I've got you."

I close my eyes, and for the first time in my life, I feel at peace because I have everything I could ever want. Bruce was right. I'm one of the lucky ones.

Epilogue

EMMETT

I go to the Plain Daisy Ranch offices to pick up Briar because this morning, I became an uncle.

Briar's waiting for me, sitting on the ledge of the brick wall, her head tilted toward the sun, one hand on her belly. Isn't my future wife the most beautiful creature?

I park and step out of my truck, walking toward her. She's working with Scarlett now as well as doing some pregnancy yoga classes. She'll run the events that don't have to do with The Knotted Barn after she has the baby. We've decided to keep the sex of the baby a surprise, so although she's far enough along to find out, we're not going to. Her ultrasound said the baby is healthy, and that's all we care about.

Gillian worked her magic, and Chad signed off all his rights to the baby. I plan on adopting him or her as soon as Briar and I get married, but the baby is already mine in my heart. I'm the one who talks to it, gives it kisses, and feeds all the cravings Briar gets. And I'd have it no other way.

"Hey, sweetheart," I say, sitting next to her. "Ready to meet the newest Noughton?"

She lowers her head and leans in to kiss my cheek. "Hey, handsome."

"Good day?" I ask.

"The best. You?"

"Yeah."

My family voted unanimously to move forward on the dude ranch idea, as well as the gender reveals and a whole umbrella of different themed retreats. But today I was helping on the ranch because Jude has his hands full. We're family, and we help each other out.

"Parker booked a divorce party." She smiles. "She left Chad, and now she wants to celebrate. I think she wants to bring the kids to meet this little one when he or she is born."

"That's great?"

She nods. "It is. I didn't know if she'd ever get there. And I definitely didn't think it'd be this soon."

"She seems like a trooper. She'll come out this all right."

"Definitely." She slips off the wall and straightens her dress. "Let's go. I don't want us to be the last ones there."

I escort her to my truck and open the passenger door for her. She climbs in and buckles up. I'll never tire of seeing her in my truck. I'm still surprised every time I come home, and she hasn't yet come to her senses and left me.

We drive to the hospital and park next to Ben's truck. Brooks is just parking his sheriff's vehicle when we walk in, so we wait for him at the entrance.

"Hey, lovebirds. How's the bun in the oven?"

Briar rolls her eyes. "How are the donuts?"

God, I fucking love her.

"Stereotypes." He shakes his head.

"So, you don't eat donuts? I heard Boston Cream is your fave," I say because it's always fun to poke Brooks.

"They are, but I'm on a diet." He pats his flat stomach.

We take the elevator up to the maternity floor, and the

doors open to the waiting room where my family is being disruptive and loud. No surprise there. They're always taking up all the space and not understanding that some conversations can be quiet. But who am I to point fingers?

"I'm an uncle!" I shout.

Briar slides by me, going to sit with all the women.

"So am I, dipshit." Ben hovers by the entrance to the waiting room. "And get ready because you're the next two who get to go in."

"Have you already seen her?" I lean into Ben, lowering my voice.

"Yes."

"Is she... you know?"

He raises his eyebrows. "What?"

"Like, an ugly baby?" I ask, as quietly as possible.

"Nah, she looks like Sadie."

We both laugh. I didn't really think Jude and Sadie could make an ugly baby, but I didn't want to be surprised. Jude would be chasing me through the halls and screaming at me if I said anything offensive.

"Briar," I call, waving her over, "we're next."

She does a little clap of her hands, and when Lottie and Romy come out, we head through the doors and down the hall.

"Room 203," Romy shouts.

We walk down the hall, trying not to peek into any rooms, but can you blame us? We'll be here soon too. We had to stop seeing Dr. Morales and find a doctor down here. It makes more sense, but if any issues arise, it is nice to have a big hospital doctor we can call.

I knock on the door of room 203 and see Sadie in the bed, Jude sitting to the side and holding Daisy.

"Hey, you two," Sadie says with a smile. "Are you ready for this?"

"I don't know. How painful is it?" Briar asks, going right to Jude and staring over his shoulder.

"You live with Emmett, so you already have a high tolerance for pain. You got this." Sadie laughs.

I flip her off quickly, so Jude doesn't see it.

Sadie only laughs harder. "Introduce her to her aunt and uncle."

Jude stands and goes to hand her to Briar.

"Oh, no, Emmett first," Briar says.

He walks over to me. "If you drop her, brothers or not, I will kill you."

"Way to put fear in me right before you hand me your most precious belonging. "And hello? I played football, too. I can cradle a baby."

Jude places Daisy in my arms. Ben wasn't lying, she definitely favors Sadie. Her curly dark blonde hair is like her mom's, and her eyes aren't as brown as ours but more of a hazel. The perfect mix between the two.

"She's adorable. Congratulations, you guys."

Briar leans over me, running her finger over Daisy's small hands. "She's precious."

"Yeah, she is." Jude's now in bed beside Sadie. He kisses her temple, and they tell us about how the delivery process was for them.

They're so in love, so happy. I look at Briar. I love Jude and Sadie, but they wasted a lot of time not being together. I don't want that for us.

"Sorry, you have to take her back," I say, handing the baby to Sadie.

Her forehead wrinkles as she takes Daisy, and she looks at Jude. "Well then. Our daughter just got slighted."

"No, no. She's perfect. Beautiful. And I'll be the best damn uncle, but I have to..." I fall to my knees in front of Briar.

"What are you doing? Are you high on baby or something?"

"I don't have a ring, and I'm completely unprepared, but I love you. And you love me, and you know how I work."

"Yes, I do. Now get up off the floor," she says quietly.

"Marry me, Briar. You hold my heart in your hands. You own it already. And I promise to keep yours safe in return. I want everything a life with you will bring. The highs. The lows. The arguments because of the make-up sex." I shrug. "I've loved your stomach growing our baby, and I love our lazy Sunday mornings. And I love our banter, the way only we can joke with one another. I'm in love with you, and I don't want to waste one more minute not being your husband. Will you marry me?"

She glances at Jude and Sadie before she turns back to me, tears in her eyes. "Of course I will."

I stand and take her head in my hands, kissing her with the promise to give her everything she wants in life.

"Congratulations, you two," Sadie says with a smile in her voice. "Great proposal, Emmett."

"Not better than mine," Jude grumbles.

"You each did your proposals in your own way. They were both perfect." Sadie places her hand on Jude's leg. "Now, go tell the whole family outside."

I don't want to remove my lips from Briar's. I really should've done this at home.

"Stop kissing. I can't have sex for six weeks. Get out," Jude says.

I end our kiss and take Briar's hand, laughing. "Ready?"

"Always."

We walk out of the room and down the hall to where everyone waits.

"Now you get to write Mrs. Emmett Noughton for real," I say.

She knocks me with her shoulder. "Keep it up, Little Noughton."

I grab her around her waist and bury my head in her neck. "You and I both know there's nothing little about me."

She laughs, and it's the best sound in the whole world. My one and only love.

EIGHT MONTHS LATER...

I roll over in bed, snuggling up to Briar in the bed of our hotel room in Vegas. Her hand runs down my arm, and her wedding ring sparkles from the sun slipping in through the curtains we forgot to close last night. No wonder, in our condition.

"My head hurts. Too much champagne and too much noise at the casino," she says.

"Yeah, we should get breakfast. And don't forget that we have to pick up our pictures today at the chapel."

We opted for a quickie Vegas wedding, but of course all our cousins decided to ambush us and come along.

Our little one is home with Grandpa and my aunts and uncles. It was hard to get Briar to leave, but we both needed the time to reconnect after the last few months with a newborn.

I groan as we get up. We shower and dress quickly, wanting to escape before any of my family members try to get us to go shopping, have breakfast with them, or the worst option, visit the Hoover Dam. That was Bennett's idea because he promised Wren he'd take pictures. At least he came. He needed a break too.

Hand in hand, we hop in a taxi to head back to the chapel we got married in yesterday. I can't believe these places are always open.

The guy who married us waves while talking to another

couple who look as though they didn't sleep at all and are still drunk.

"Oh, I wonder if we're on here." Briar goes over to a screen displaying pictures of couples who got married here.

We wait as the pictures flip from one couple to the next. Some are dressed in traditional wedding dresses and tuxedos, others in cargo shorts, crop tops, and red eyes. And ones like us. Briar wore a pretty ivory dress that flowed over her curves, and I wore slacks and a button-down. No tie and no jacket.

"There we are!" Briar points.

Sure enough, we're facing one another with our hands clasped, smiling wide. I tug her to my side, and we watch a few more pictures of us walking down the aisle and smiling with one another, then some with my cousins in them.

"Newlyweds," Roger, the guy who works here, says. "Survived the first night. Consider this marriage a success." He laughs. He made jokes like that the entire time. "Just kidding. This one couple that came in last night." He blows out a breath. "They were arguing minutes after the nuptials were done. Those two won't last, let me tell you."

"Oh, that's awful," Briar says.

"Yeah, the guy kept talking about a donut place, and the bride had just had it. Then the next minute, they're kissing and falling into the back of a taxi. Who knows, maybe that love-hate thing will work out for them." He glances at the screen and laughs. "Oh, that's them." He leans in for a better look. "Definitely drunk."

We look at the screen, and Briar gasps while I stand there wide-eyed. A picture of a very drunk Lottie and Brooks is plastered on the screen. Lottie has a veil on, and they're holding hands and walking down the aisle.

"Those were our guests!" Briar steps closer. "But they weren't wearing those outfits during our ceremony."

"They came around eleven or so."

Briar's nose is practically on the screen.

"Kind of cool, you share an anniversary with them." Roger smiles.

Jesus. I thought we were done with secrets. I shouldn't be trusted with this information.

The End

Also by Piper Rayne

Plain Daisy Ranch

One Last Summer (FREE Prequel)

The One I Left Behind

The One I Stood Beside

The One I Didn't See Coming

C.F. - Plain Daisy Ranch #4 (title coming)

The Baileys

Lessons from a One-Night Stand (FREE)

Advice from a Jilted Bride

Birth of a Baby Daddy

Operation Bailey Wedding (Novella)

Falling for My Brother's Best Friend

Demise of a Self-Centered Playboy

Confessions of a Naughty Nanny

Operation Bailey Babies (Novella)

Secrets of the World's Worst Matchmaker

Winning my Best Friend's Girl

Rules for Dating Your Ex

Operation Bailey Birthday (Novella)

The Greene Family

My Twist of Fortune (Free Prequel)

My Beautiful Neighbor (FREE)

My Almost Ex

My Vegas Groom

A Greene Family Summer Bash (Novella)

My Sister's Flirty Friend

My Unexpected Surprise

My Famous Frenemy

A Greene Family Vacation (Novella)

My Scorned Best Friend

My Fake Fiancé

My Brother's Forbidden Friend

A Greene Family Christmas (Novella)

Lake Starlight

The Problem with Second Chances

The Issue with Bad Boy Roommates

The Trouble with Runaway Brides

The Drawback of Single Dads

Modern Love

Charmed by the Bartender

Hooked by the Boxer

Mad about the Banker

Single Dads Club

Real Deal

Dirty Talker

Sexy Beast

Hollywood Hearts

Mister Mom

Animal Attraction

Domestic Bliss

Bedroom Games

Cold as Ice

On Thin Ice

Break the Ice

Chicago Law

Smitten with the Best Man

Tempted by my Ex-Husband

Seduced by my Ex's Divorce Attorney

Blue Collar Brothers

Flirting with Fire

Crushing on the Cop

Engaged to the EMT

White Collar Brothers

Sexy Filthy Boss

Dirty Flirty Enemy

Wild Steamy Hook-up

The Rooftop Crew

My Bestie's Ex

A Royal Mistake

The Rival Roomies

Our Star-Crossed Kiss

The Do-Over

A Co-Workers Crush

Hockey Hotties

Countdown to a Kiss (Free Prequel)

My Lucky #13 (FREE)

The Trouble with #9

Faking it with #41

Tropical Hat Trick (Novella)

Sneaking around with #34

Second Shot with #76

Offside with #55

Kingsmen Football Stars

False Start (Free Prequel)

You Had Your Chance, Lee Burrows

You Can't Kiss the Nanny, Brady Banks

Over My Brother's Dead Body, Chase Andrews

Chicago Grizzlies

On the Defense (Free Prequel)

Something like Hate

Something like Lust

Something like Love

The Nest

Mr. Heartbreaker

Mr. B (Title to be revealed)

Mr. S (Title to be revealed)

Mr. C (Title to be revealed)

Holiday Romances

Single and Ready to Jingle

Claus and Effect

Merry Kissmas

Cockamamie Unicorn Ramblings

Oh, Emmett, he was one of the characters who landed on the page easily. The problem with a character like him is it's hard to find the real person underneath. Sure, they can steal a scene in someone else's book, but how do we write *their* book?

We were worried, but Emmett peeled back his layers pretty quickly. The youngest who can't remember his mother, growing up with a dad and two brothers. He brought humor to most situations to tame the seriousness from all the testosterone.

When we first plotted out the first three books, Briar's name was actually going to be Rowan. But we changed it to Briar while writing The One I Left Behind because we have another character we want to name Rowan (you'll find out soon). We hadn't planned to set Emmett up with Gillian's sister, in fact we had a whole other idea in mind for who his heroine might be, but when we were writing book one we knew that she would be the one for Emmett. Who doesn't love the forbidden aspect of their dynamic, right?

Once we settled on Briar we knew she was going to be fresh off a break-up with a guy who she found out was married. But it wasn't until we were plotting that we decided she'd be pregnant with that man's baby, too.

The real change in this book happened at four in the afternoon the day of our deadline (the book was due at 9 o'clock) when we decided that Parker's husband was going to be Chad (the married man/baby daddy). We talked through it, unsure if we could swing it. So much of the book had already been written, which meant some changes. But in the end, we loved the surprise it would give the readers, so we made it happen. And we still made our deadline (well, maybe an hour late).

Writing these three brothers have been so much fun. Their fights, their bets, their picking on one another. The cemetery scenes (family meetings), Bruce and his Saturday night guests. And we promise this is not the end for them. You'll see them in the next set of Plain Daisy Ranch books, but next we'll be concentrating on Darla's kids. And of course, Lottie Owens is up first!

As always, we have a lot of people to thank for getting this book into your hands...

Nina and the entire Valentine PR team. The organization, the promotion, the way you keep us on point with deadlines. We appreciate you SO much!

Cassie from Joy Editing for line edits who still took our book an hour late. LOL, but is always willing to work with us on extensions.

Ellie from My Brother's Editor for line edits and proofing. We give you barely any time, but you always come through.

Hang Le for the cover and branding for the entire series which is beyond gorgeous. You're talent and eye is unmatched, always making our characters come to life.

Regina Wamba for the breathtaking photo, giving us the inspiration for Emmett and Briar. They are perfect in every way. Your talent amazes us.

All the bloggers who choose to read us with so many options out there. We are appreciative and honored to be on your list of must reads and love reading all your reviews, edits and more.

All the Piper Rayne Unicorns who support us every day, all day. We'd be lost without you answering our polls and telling us what you love and hate. We strive to give you the best Piper Rayne experience and we can't say much else except that you're awesome.

Readers who have an abundance of books to choose from. Thank you for picking up one of ours. We do hope you enjoyed the story.

What's next for Plain Daisy Ranch? We're going to switch over to the Bruce's sister, Darla's family, The Owens. Don't worry, these Noughton brothers are only on the other side of the ranch, and you'll get plenty of cameos. What would we do without our softball games, Fourth of July parties, and hang-outs at The Hidden Cave? See you there.

xo,
Piper & Rayne

About Piper & Rayne

Piper Rayne is a *USA Today* Bestselling Author duo who write "heartwarming humor with a side of sizzle" about families, whether that be blood or found. They both have e-readers full of one-clickable books, they're married to husbands who drive them to drink, and they're both chauffeurs to their kids. Most of all, they love hot heroes and quirky heroines who make them laugh, and they hope you do, too!

Printed in Great Britain
by Amazon

51800754R00162